'Before we set off,' said Julian, heaving the rucksack on to his back, 'we had better zip up our tents!' There was one tent for the boys and another for the girls. Timmy generally swapped from one to the other – according to his mood! When the tents had been securely zipped up, they discussed which direction they should head in for the railway line. The trouble was, they all had different ideas. Julian thought it would be one way, while Dick thought another. George thought they should go north, while Anne thought south. Even Timmy seemed to have a preference of his own.

To decide whose idea to follow, throw the special FAMOUS FIVE DICE. If you throw mystery, you must take that route instead.

JULIAN thrown	go to 166
DICK thrown	go to 79
GEORGE thrown	go to 35
ANNE thrown	go to 146
TIMMY thrown	go to 61
MYSTERY thrown	go to 248

They came across a large rock, sticking upright from the ground. They were just about to walk round it when Julian noticed some strange writing scratched into the lichen. 'It looks like some sort of code,' he said excitedly. Then he had another thought. Maybe it had something to do with the railway line! They hurriedly searched through their rucksacks for a codebook.

Use your CODEBOOK CARD to find out what the message said by decoding the instruction below. If you don't have a CODEBOOK in your RUCKSACK, go to 60 instead.

The signpost didn't point to the railway line after all, however. It merely said *DEVILS' HILL* one way and *GREAT TOR* the other. 'Well, at least we now know it wasn't worth getting our feet wet for!' laughed Dick, as they just had to guess the direction. ***Go to 132.***

4

They thought they should have reached the far end of the tunnel by now and were becoming worried that they had got lost again. To save them wasting time, Dick suggested that he run ahead and find out whether it was the right way or not. If it was, he would let them know by holding up one hand. If it wasn't, he would hold up two. So he hurried off but he had become so small by the time he sent back the signal that the others weren't sure whether it was one hand he was holding up or both. They were so puzzled that they forgot all about their binoculars for a while. Then Anne suddenly remembered them, quickly searching through her rucksack.

Use your BINOCULARS CARD to read Dick's signal by placing exactly over the shape below – then follow the instruction. If you don't have any BINOCULARS, go to 82 instead.

(G GN : O .KJH   RFRE   T K   O .
W : I F : ,J.M   GBNJ?O M U IU: RUB
    JKLZ ON MBHUGF UUY!(KJH   B E
T W   JBMK   HGJ(?   SGJ:L   K.M.F   O

Suddenly, though, they heard a rumble along the track and they all fled in different directions! 'What babies we all are!' said Julian when they had finally come together again. 'It was probably just some tractor crossing the track further up.' Before they went much further along the line, however, they decided to have some of their picnic. After a shock like that, they all felt they needed it!

Take one PICNIC CARD from your LUNCHBOX. Now go to 172.

Hoping to find out what they were up to, The Five then began following the men. On the way, George's tummy suddenly started making loud gurgling noises! 'Ssh!' whispered the others, 'or they'll hear us.' But George's tummy just wouldn't keep quiet, becoming louder and louder. They decided the only solution was to let her have a quick bite to eat.

Take one PICNIC CARD from your LUNCHBOX. Now go to 113.

They suddenly heard a rough-sounding voice from behind. 'What do you think you lot are doing here?' it asked, making them jump. 'Come to spy on our little treasures, have you?' When they turned round, they saw that there were three surly-looking men standing there. The next thing they knew, the men had grabbed hold of them, forcing them against the wall. 'Well, we'll just have to make sure you stay here until the operation's over,' one of them said. He began to tie them up while the others loaded the crates on to the trucks. As soon as they had finished, the men left them there, closing the sliding wall again so they were sealed in! *Go to 29.*

8

They all suddenly froze as they heard a loud rumbling noise. 'It must be the ghost train!' shrieked Anne, dropping her lunchbox. But then they realised that the noise was coming from the bricked-up part in front of them, which was slowly beginning to slide open. 'Gosh,' said Dick, 'we must have trodden on some sort of secret mechanism in the ground!' Bending down to pick up her lunchbox, Anne found that the lid had come open and some of her sandwiches had rolled into the dirt.

Take one PICNIC CARD from your LUNCHBOX. Now go to 140.

9

They were able to decode some of the message but the most important part was lost under a burnt bit. Without it, the rest didn't really make much sense. Stepping down from the engine, they then went to investigate one of the trucks. It was full of large crates and so they climbed in to have a better look. 'Gosh,' said George, as they opened one of them up, 'it's packed with valuable silverware!' She was so distracted by all this treasure that she didn't notice Timmy pinch one of her sandwiches!

Take one PICNIC CARD from your LUNCHBOX. Now go to 70.

10

'We had better run for a while,' said Julian as they were about to set off, 'or we're never going to reach the farmhouse in time.' They had been running for quite a way when Dick suddenly dived to the ground. It sounded as if someone had shot at him! But then he realised that it was just his ginger beer. All that running had fizzed it up and made it explode!

Take one PICNIC CARD from your LUNCHBOX. Now go to 74.

The coded message said that they were exactly half way up the shaft. 'Is that all?' complained George, giving Timmy another tired push. 'I thought we'd be nearly at the top by now!' **Go to 160.**

12

They were just opening their maps when Jock heard a loud squeal not too far away. 'That's Gerty, one of our pigs!' he cried. 'There's no need to use the map after all!' They were in such a hurry to cross the bridge that Dick tripped and accidentally flung his lunchbox into the water below. It sank slowly to the bottom!

Take one PICNIC CARD from your LUNCHBOX. Now go to 116.

13

The map showed that they *were* heading in the right direction and so Anne felt much more relieved. They hadn't gone much further when she suddenly had to shout at the driver to stop – there was a sheep sitting in the middle of the track! As they quickly helped it to one side, Dick noticed a codebook underneath it in the mud. He decided to take it with them in case it could be of use.

If you don't already have one, put the CODEBOOK CARD into your RUCKSACK. Now go to 93.

Quite a long way further on their journey, Timmy suddenly stopped. 'What's wrong?' asked the others as his nose started to twitch. Then they realised. Coming over the next ridge was a sudden mist! Within seconds it had surrounded them and they couldn't see more than a yard in front. To begin with, they all felt their way through it in a close group, but then Julian suggested one of them should take the lead to make sure it was safe.

Throw the FAMOUS FIVE DICE to decide who it is to be.

JULIAN thrown	go to 106
DICK thrown	go to 261
GEORGE thrown	go to 214
ANNE thrown	go to 168
TIMMY thrown	go to 119
MYSTERY thrown	go to 133

'Let's just hope nobody comes the other way!' said Julian as he led them higher and higher up the narrow path. It seemed unlikely, however. They hadn't seen so much as one other person on the moors so far. Just to check there was no one coming from the other end, though, Julian suggested having a look through their binoculars.

Use your BINOCULARS CARD to see if there's anyone

coming by placing exactly over the shape below – then follow the instruction. If you don't have any BINOCULARS in your RUCKSACK, go to 81 instead.

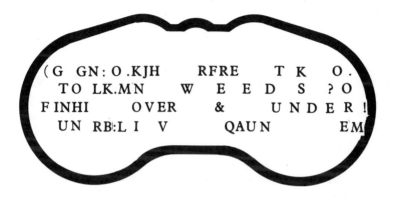

(G GN: O .KJH   RFRE   T K   O .
   TO LK.MN   W   E   E   D   S   ? O
F INHI   OVER   &   U N D E R !
   UN RB:L I   V   QAU N   E M

16

They didn't have to go south for long before Julian spotted some rusting sheds in the distance. Then, as they went nearer, Dick noticed some heaps of coal as well. 'It's a railway yard!' they all cheered. 'This must be the beginning of the line.' Scarcely able to contain their excitement, they hurried towards it.

Hurry with them to 249.

17

Julian's compass showed that they were facing south. So, as long as they made sure they kept to that direction, they should be going in a straight line. Suddenly, Anne screamed! For a moment she thought she had gone over a steep drop, but it was just something she tripped on. They felt the ground to see what it was. 'Look, a pair of binoculars!' exclaimed George. They decided they would hand them in to the police station when they returned. In the meantime, though, they might well be useful!

If you don't already have it, put the BINOCULARS CARD into your RUCKSACK. Now go to 36.

18

When they were back at the top of the hill, Anne noticed some large flat stones forming a square in the grass. She asked Julian what they were for. 'They were put here in the old days,' he replied, 'and were for lighting beacons on to send messages.' He added that if they looked closely they could probably still see where they were charred. That wasn't all they were able to see. On one of them, there was also a coded message! They began to search for their codebooks.

Use your CODEBOOK CARD to find out what this message said by decoding the instruction below. If you don't have one, go to 42.

The coded inscription said that the tunnel could be seen by climbing the steps. They wondered what steps it was talking about but then they found a small door at the back of the monument. Inside, there was a stone staircase and it led all the way to an open platform at the top! 'Yes, there's the other end!' they all cried, as they pointed to where the railway came out again in a dip between the hills. ***Go to 136.***

20

Just before they reached the tunnel's other end, Timmy started to sniff around an old rabbit hole. 'Oh, leave it alone, Timmy,' the others insisted as he pushed in his muzzle, 'we've got much more important things to do!' But Timmy pushed his nose in even further, eventually pulling out an old book that someone must have stuffed down the hole. The others guessed it must be quite important if the person had gone to so much trouble to hide it – and indeed it was. It was for decoding secret messages!

If you don't already have it, put the CODEBOOK CARD into your RUCKSACK. Now go to 155.

21

Julian just touched the train first, climbing into the engine. 'Here's our ghost train,' he exclaimed, 'but it looks perfectly real to me!' Jock jumped on board as well. 'So this is what I saw from my bedroom window!' he said. But he still couldn't understand why it was making these midnight trips. Nor could the others. Walking round the trucks, Dick suddenly noticed a coded message that someone had written into the dust. He hurriedly looked for his codebook, thinking this might throw some light on the mystery.

Use your CODEBOOK CARD to find out what the message said by decoding the instruction below. If you don't have one, go to 191 instead.

22

The men started walking further up the line and so The Five decided to follow them to see what they were up to. They all went very quietly to make sure they didn't attract their attention. If they were as mean as they sounded, they were likely to be a lot of trouble! ***Go to 113.***

23

Dick carried the lamp in front of him, the others following right behind. They weren't able to go far along this branch-line, however, before it suddenly ended. It looked as if it had once continued through a large arch in the wall but that arch was now bricked-up. They were just about to turn back when George noticed a message chalked on to the tunnel roof. Unfortunately, it was so far above that they couldn't read it, but then Dick had an idea! 'Let's use our binoculars,' he said, beginning to search through his rucksack.

Use your BINOCULARS CARD to make this message bigger by placing exactly over the shape below — then follow the instruction. If you don't have one, go to 252 instead.

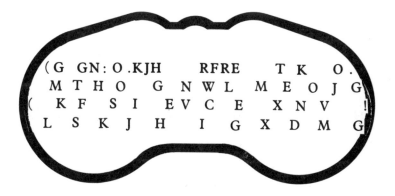

```
(G  GN: O .KJH      RFRE      T  K     O .
   M  T  H  O    G  N W L    M  E  O  J  G
(  K  F   S  I    E V C  E     X  N  V        !
   L   S  K  J   H     I   G  X  D  M      G
```

24

It was Timmy who picked the shortest blade, drawing it with his teeth, and so he led the way into the tunnel. He didn't really mind going first, though. In fact, he thought it was only right since he was the dog! He hadn't gone far into the tunnel when he suddenly pricked up his ears. He could hear someone coming after them from back down the line. 'Why, it's Jock!' they all shouted with glee as they saw who it was. 'What are you doing here?' Jock told them that his stepfather had gone into town for the rest of the day and so he had run along to join them. Guessing that they might want to explore the tunnel, he had also brought a lamp. 'But how did you get here so quickly?' George asked. He replied that there was a short cut via 'Little Lake', and asked if they had a map so that he could show them.

Use your MAP CARD to find out which square the lake is in — then follow the instruction. If you don't have one, you'll have to guess which instruction to follow.

If you think E2	go to 241
If you think E3	go to 265
If you think E1	go to 71

25

But they couldn't see a fire-bucket anywhere. 'Someone must have taken it,' said Julian as they sat down to eat some of their picnic. They thought it might cheer them up a bit!

Take one PICNIC CARD from your LUNCHBOX. Now go to 221. (Remember: when there are no picnic cards left in your lunchbox, the game is over and you must start again.)

26

They felt much better now they knew exactly where the shaft came out and they started climbing a little faster. George and Julian also seemed to have got the knack of helping Timmy up the rungs. George suddenly put her hand on a small ledge, feeling some sort of book. 'Why, it's a codebook!' she exclaimed, taking it with her in case it was a different type to theirs.

If you don't already have it, put the CODEBOOK CARD into your RUCKSACK. Go to 31.

They worked out the man's name as *Bill Higgins*. 'Well, that's one thief we know about,' said Julian, 'but, for the others, we're going to have to make sure we catch them in the act.' So they hurriedly started off again. **Go to 116.**

They worked out the name as *Sid Sykes*. 'We'll take the gun with us to give to the police,' said Julian, putting it into his rucksack. Just before they started off again, however, they noticed something else lying in the heather. It was a compass! They decided to take this with them as well in case they needed a spare.

If you don't already have it, put the COMPASS CARD into your RUCKSACK. Go to 162.

'What are we going to do?' George asked anxiously, but then she realised that the men had forgotten Timmy. He could bite through their ropes with his sharp teeth! As soon as they were free, they tried to push the sliding wall open again but it wouldn't move. Then Anne noticed a chalked message at the very top of the arch. *'TO OPEN THE WALL FROM THE INSIDE OF THE*

CAVERN. . .' it began but the remainder was too small to read. 'I know,' said Dick, 'let's look through our binoculars!'

Use your BINOCULARS CARD to read the rest of the message by placing exactly over the shape below. If you don't have one, go to 52 instead.

```
( G  GN: O .KJH     RFRE      T K    O .
T W   ?JNM:O MNI: N S     JBMK E  OI!
T RFYH    W FRO?    QAUHT       :ITR O
F,  F MNI:  O :LNV.U  EWQ    .KJHG R  F
```

30
They were just about to take their compasses out when George noticed Jim's tyre tracks in the ground. All they had to do was follow them instead! They were so pleased with their find that they decided to have some of their ginger beer on the way.

Take one PICNIC CARD from your LUNCHBOX. Now go to 116. (Remember: when there are no picnic cards left in your lunchbox, the game is over and you must start again.)

31
They finally reached the top of the shaft, climbing out on to the heather. They must have been in the cavern longer than they thought because it had now grown quite dark. 'We'd better hurry,' said Julian, 'or we're never going to fetch the police in time. The

train will probably be driven out in an hour or two.' Jock said that the best thing to do was to go back to his farm and use the phone. The trouble was – which way was the farm? It was becoming so difficult to see that even Jock wasn't sure! The Five then all had a think, each coming up with a different suggestion.

Throw the FAMOUS FIVE DICE to decide whose suggestion to follow.

JULIAN thrown	go to 195
DICK thrown	go to 76
GEORGE thrown	go to 164
ANNE thrown	go to 245
TIMMY thrown	go to 143
MYSTERY thrown	go to 127

32

There wasn't time to look for their binoculars, though, because they suddenly heard a loud rumbling along the line. The train was coming already! They all rushed down the embankment to hide, Julian being in such a hurry that he dropped his lunchbox on the way. 'You'll just have to leave it,' said the sergeant, worried that he might otherwise give them away.

Take one PICNIC CARD from your LUNCHBOX. Now go to 212. (Remember: when there are no picnic cards left in your lunchbox, the game is over and you must start again.)

33

Using their compasses to tell the driver which way to turn, The Five soon had the van back on the track again. 'It's a good job we didn't encounter any mires,' the sergeant said with relief, 'or we would have had no end of trouble!'. *Go to 78.*

34

It was decided that Julian should sit in the front and he directed the driver along the rough, bumpy track. Suddenly, though, the track divided and Julian couldn't remember which branch to take. Had they turned right when they had come this way last time or left? Just as the sergeant was taking yet another look at his watch, Dick had an idea. They could try and spot the tunnel through their binoculars.

*Use your **BINOCULARS CARD** to make this search by placing exactly over the shape below – then follow the instruction. If you don't have one, go to 247 instead.*

```
G  GN : O .KJH      RFRE       T  K    O .
O  T MNH    HGFR W          EU:,J.  O  E
S NKMH       I ,MN              BG X  ED
FDS E  HGF    I   M   G Y!(    H  H  XDF T
```

35

At last agreeing on George's idea, the others followed her along an old pony track towards the next hill. She said that it was much higher than their hill and it would make it a lot easier to see. She was absolutely right! When they finally reached the top, they could see nearly the whole of the moors spread out beneath them. And there, in the far distance, was the old railway line! But then Julian realised there was a problem. It was all very well being able to spot the railway line from up here but how would they remember where it was when they had to go down again? Suddenly, Dick had an idea! They could use a compass to find out which direction it was in and then they would know which way to walk whether they could still see it or not.

*Use your **COMPASS CARD** to find out which direction to take by placing exactly over the shape below — and with the pointer touching north. Then go to the number that appears in the window. If you don't have a **COMPASS CARD** in your **RUCKSACK**, you'll have to guess which number to go to.*

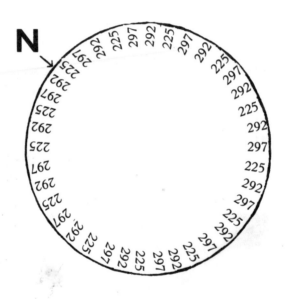

Finally, the mist cleared, disappearing as quickly as it had come. Timmy gave a happy wag of his tail. At last he could look out for rabbits again. He would still have been able to smell them, of course, but it wasn't so much fun unless you could actually see them! Out of the mist had appeared some sort of long shed in the distance. They all wondered what it was, hurriedly looking for their binoculars.

Use your BINOCULARS CARD to find out what the shed was by placing exactly over the shape below — then follow the instruction. If you don't have any BINOCULARS in your RUCKSACK, go to 80 instead.

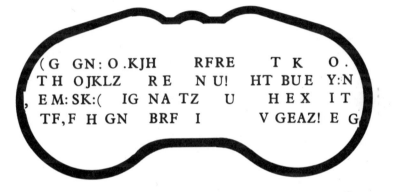

```
( G  GN: O .KJH      RFRE       T K     O .
T H OJKLZ    RE    N U!   HT BU E   Y:N
 E M: SK:(   IG NA TZ    U    H E X    I T
  TF,F H GN   BRF   I        V GEAZ! E G
```

37

They had only just started looking for their binoculars when Timmy suddenly appeared from behind. He must have been waiting for them all along! With George keeping a firm hand on him this time, they continued on their way. *Go to 2.*

38

'Look, how strange!' remarked George, suddenly pointing to some large boulders not far to their right. One was standing upright and the other lay flat across it like a huge mushroom. 'They're quite common in this area,' said Julian, explaining how they were formed thousands of years ago. He then had an idea. The boulders would probably be shown on the map and it would be a clue to where they were.

Use your MAP CARD to find out which square the mushroom-shaped boulders are in – then follow the instruction. If you don't have a MAP in your RUCKSACK, you'll have to guess which instruction to follow.

If you think A3	go to 118
If you think B2	go to 95
If you think B3	go to 304

39

The coded message was addressed to a person called *Bill* and said that they were to meet at the tunnel. 'I wonder if it's talking about the railway tunnel?' asked Anne excitedly. If it was, then there was obviously something very strange going on there after all. It only made them more eager than ever to find the line! ***Go to 132.***

40

The coded message said that the goods would be collected at the level crossing. They wondered what goods it was talking about – and why someone had made such a mystery about it! Well, one thing was for certain. If there *was* a mystery to be solved, they'd be the ones who would solve it! They had always been successful before. 'Woof!' barked Timmy loudly, as if he was thinking exactly the same. ***Go to 172.***

41

'Dick's only showing one hand,' Anne cried with joy as she looked through her binoculars, 'that means it must be the right way!' And, when they caught Dick up, they saw that it was. For, there in front of them was the railway line again – and the other end of the tunnel. They had found it at last! ***Go to 155.***

42

They were all suddenly distracted by a loud bark from Timmy. 'What is it, you stupid ol' thing?' asked Julian, but then he noticed what Timmy was looking at. It was the other end of the tunnel – and it was right beneath them! They hurried down the slope towards it, sliding on the short grass. George suddenly started going so fast, however, that she went head over heels. She picked herself up at the bottom with a grumpy look. She was fine herself but her bottle of ginger beer had broken.

Take one PICNIC CARD from your LUNCHBOX before continuing to 155.

43

'*FOR TRAVELLERS WHO SEEK THE RAILWAY TUNNEL
. . .*' the coded message began, but that was as much as they could
work out. The rest of the inscription was too worn to read. When
they had walked a few steps further round the base of the
monument, however, they discovered another inscription. And
this one was in plain English! '*RAILWAY TUNNEL IS IN
STRAIGHT LINE FROM STATUE'S POINTING FINGER,*'it
read. They wondered which statue it was talking about but, finally,
they found it. It was straight above them – at the top of the
monument! Now they knew which way to go, they decided to have
a quick sandwich or two before setting off.

**Take one PICNIC CARD from your LUNCHBOX. Now
go to 136.**

44

A compass wasn't really necessary, however, because "east" was
marked by a small arrow at the foot of the monument. On the way,
Dick thought it would be a good idea to check their route on the
map. But when he looked for his map in his rucksack, he found
that it was missing! It must have dropped out at the monument
when he was searching for his compass. Since it was much too far
to walk back, they decided they would just have to leave it.

**If you have one, take the MAP CARD from your
RUCKSACK. Now go to 4.**

Timmy insisted that he go first, wagging his tail all the way to the top of the track. When they reached the top, they expected to see where the railway came out again but it was nowhere in sight. Either it was hidden in a dip - or the tunnel ran for miles and miles! They had only gone a little further along the hilltop when Dick noticed a small tablet of stone sticking up from the heather. It was like an old milestone, with some writing on it. *'OTHER END OF TUNNEL IS HALF A MILE TO THE EAST'* it read. Dick excitedly looked for his compass.

*Use your **COMPASS CARD** to find which direction to head in by placing exactly over the shape below — and with pointer touching north. Then go to the number that appears in the window. If you don't have one, you'll have to guess which number to go to.*

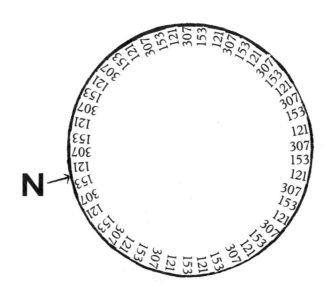

'I think it's time for some of our picnic,' said Anne when they must have been about half-way there. The others willingly accepted her suggestion, searching for a nice piece of dry ground. George then ate her way through more than half her sandwiches. 'If there are any ghosts to be encountered,' she said through a mouthful of bread, 'I'd better make sure I'm strong enough!'

Take one PICNIC CARD from your LUNCHBOX. Now go to 186.

They had only gone a short way further along the tunnel when they noticed that part of the line branched off to the left. Not only that, but it looked a lot shinier than the rest, as if it had been used fairly recently! Curious, they decided to explore this branch. 'I bet it has something to do with the ghost train,' said Julian excitedly.

Throw the FAMOUS FIVE DICE to decide who is to take the lead on this exploration.

JULIAN thrown	go to 101
DICK thrown	go to 23
GEORGE thrown	go to 159
ANNE thrown	go to 192
TIMMY thrown	go to 69
MYSTERY thrown	go to 242

48

The coded message said that the crates were hidden under the canvas sheet in the corner. They wondered which crates it was talking about but there was only one way to find out – to go and have a look! 'Gosh,' said Dick, pulling the canvas back, 'they're full of valuable silverware!' At the back of the crates, they also found an old map of the area. Shaking off the dust, they decided to take it with them.

If you don't already have it, put the MAP CARD into your RUCKSACK. Now go to 7.

49

Having found the fire-bucket, they measured out the ten paces. They came to a loose slab in the floor and, lifting it up, they saw a small lever underneath. But when they pulled it, nothing happened! 'They must have switched off the mechanism,' sighed George, 'just in case we discovered it.' Their search for it wasn't a complete waste of time, however, for also under the slab was a codebook. Since it looked different to theirs, they decided to take it.

If you don't already have it, put the CODEBOOK CARD into your RUCKSACK. Now go to 221.

50

The coded message said that the arch could be opened by pushing the eighth brick to the right. Not really believing it, they gave the brick a firm press. They watched, open-mouthed, as the whole of the bricked-up part suddenly began to move! *Go to 140.*

51

Unfortunately, it was Anne who drew the shortest blade of grass and so she nervously led the way into the tunnel. Dick and Julian offered to take her place but she thought it only fair to keep to the draw. Suddenly, they heard a loud voice behind them! 'Why, it's Jock!' they all shouted with delight as he came running into the tunnel after them. 'What are you doing here?' Jock explained that his stepfather had gone into town for the rest of the day and so he had come to join their adventure. Knowing that they might want to explore the tunnel, he had also brought a lamp with him. Feeling a lot happier now that she could see properly, Anne continued to move forward. She had only gone a little way further when the lamp lit up a scrap of paper between the rails. Picking it up, she saw that it was in some sort of code.

*Use your **CODEBOOK CARD** to find out what this scrap of paper said by decoding the instruction below. If you don't have one, go to 71 instead.*

52

Julian said it would be a lot quicker, though, for one of them to stand on his shoulders to read the message. It was agreed that it should be Anne, since she was the lightest. He helped her up, cupping her foot in his hands. *'TO OPEN THE WALL FROM THE INSIDE OF THE CAVERN,'* she read out when she was at the right level, *'PRESS THE BUTTON ONE METRE FURTHER UP.'* Even standing on Julian's shoulders, though, it was much too high for her to reach. 'If only we had a long pole,' said Dick disappointedly but then he had another idea. He could try and hit the button with his codebook. On the very first throw, however, the codebook landed on a ledge and now they couldn't reach that either!

If you have one, take the CODEBOOK CARD from your RUCKSACK. Now go to 221.

53
It wasn't long before Timmy had picked up the scent again and they were able to put their compasses away. 'What would we do without him!' exclaimed George as she proudly followed her pet across the heather. *Go to 74.*

54
Jock didn't need any binoculars, though, because an outside light suddenly went on and he recognised their barn. 'Yes, it *is* our farm!' he shouted eagerly as he led the way. To make it easier to run, Dick quickly finished off his ginger beer. But it only meant that, instead of his lunchbox feeling heavy, it was now his tummy!

Take one PICNIC CARD from your LUNCHBOX. Now go to 116.

55
They followed their compasses back into the cavern again. 'Here it is!' said George, finding the rope under an up-turned box. Julian quickly knotted one end into a sort of seat, placing Timmy inside. It worked perfectly! They now returned to the shaft, climbing it in stages as they hauled Timmy up after them.

Keep climbing to 160.

George climbed first, with Timmy wedged between her and Julian so they could help him up. George pulled, while Julian pushed. 'What a pity Timmy can't grip the rungs like us,' George said exhaustedly. They had climbed a little further when Jock noticed an inscription chiselled into the brickwork. *'THIS SHAFT COMES OUT MID-WAY BETWEEN THE CAIRN AND THE MONUMENT',* it read. 'It must have been inscribed by one of the men who built the shaft,' said Dick as they all started searching for their maps. They found the cairn easily – but where was the monument?

*Use your **MAP CARD** to find out which square the monument is in – then follow the instruction. If you don't have one, you'll have to guess which instruction to follow.*

If you think D3	go to 31
If you think E3	go to 178
If you think E4	go to 26

But there wasn't enough light in the van and the maps were too difficult to read. Dick suggested that they should stop and hold the map in front of the van's headlights but the sergeant said it would waste too much time. So they just had to hope they were going the right way after all! ***Go to 93.***

That very same moment, however, they heard a rumbling sound
further along the line. They jumped behind the embankment so
quickly that Julian dropped his lunchbox on the line. 'You'll just
have to leave it there,' said the sergeant, worried that he might be
seen.

*Take one PICNIC CARD from your LUNCHBOX. Now
go to 212.* (Remember: when there are no picnic cards left in your
lunchbox, the game is over and you must start again.)

Julian held firmly to the back of Anne's anorak to make sure she
didn't fall. 'Are you sure you don't want someone else to go first?'
he asked as she continued slowly forward. But she said that she
didn't, forcing herself to be brave. Anyway, it was only a few
hundred yards before the path dropped again and it joined a wide
farm track much further down. 'What's this for?' asked George, at
length, as they came across a shallow pit with some iron bars across
the top. 'It's called a sheep grid,' Julian answered, 'and it's to stop
sheep straying from one part of the track to another.' He also
thought of another use for it. It would help show them where they
were on the map!

*Use your MAP CARD to find out which square the sheep
grid is in – then follow the instruction. If you don't have a
MAP in your RUCKSACK, you'll have to guess which
instruction to follow.*

If you think C2	go to 270
If you think A2	go to 216
If you think B1	go to 299

They were still hunting for their codebooks when Timmy suddenly gave a loud bark. 'What is it?' the others asked, following where he was pointing. Then they realised. Some way in the distance were a number of large, rusting sheds. It was a railway yard! 'This must be where the line starts,' said Julian excitedly, as they hurried towards it. In fact, they were in such a hurry that Dick dropped his lunchbox on the way. What was worse, the lid came open and some of his sandwiches rolled into the mud.

Take one PICNIC CARD from your LUNCHBOX before continuing to 249.

'Okay, Timmy, we'll all go your way,' they finally agreed as he strained in the direction of a small river. They followed the river for a good mile or more but there still wasn't a railway line in sight. 'Are you sure you didn't come this way just because you liked the water, Timmy?' Julian asked with a chuckle. But George quickly came to her dog's defence. She didn't like him being laughed at – even as a joke. 'If Timmy says it's this direction, then it *is* this direction!' she insisted firmly. And just to prove it, she pointed out a small bridge ahead. She said that they could look it up on the map if they didn't believe her.

Use your MAP CARD to find out which square the bridge is in – then follow the instruction. If you don't have a MAP in your RUCKSACK, you'll have to guess which instruction to follow.

If you think E1	go to 280
If you think B1	go to 269
If you think C1	go to 117

62

To save them looking for their compasses, however, the artist pointed which direction south was. They showed how grateful they were by offering him some of their picnic. 'Mmm, that would be wonderful,' the artist replied, 'I haven't eaten all day!' After leaving him two sandwiches of cheese and one of meat paste, they continued on their way.

Take one PICNIC CARD from your LUNCHBOX. Now go to 16.

63

Anne was still so busy thinking about those lovely ponies that she tripped on a rock hidden in the grass. As she was picking herself up again, her hand touched a curious shape. Parting the undergrowth, she found that it was an old codebook! They decided to take it with them in case it might be useful.

If you don't already have it, put the CODEBOOK CARD into your RUCKSACK. Now go to 38.

64

'Do you think Sam was just trying to put us off?' asked Dick as they all followed George down the centre of the track. Julian wasn't so sure. The caretaker's frightened voice certainly *sounded* genuine enough. Timmy suddenly started to sniff at a marker sign at the side of the rail. 'Leave it alone, Timmy,' said George, 'it's just to tell train drivers to slow down for the yard.' But Timmy continued to sniff at the post, as if he thought there was something suspicious about it. The others went to have a closer look. Timmy was right – on the back of the sign someone had pencilled a coded message!

Use your CODEBOOK CARD to find out what this

message said by decoding the instruction below. If you don't have one, go to 263 instead.

65

Unfortunately the mire wasn't shown on the map. Since they didn't really fancy crossing it, they decided to return up the hill. But, before they began, they had a quick drink of their ginger beer.

Take one PICNIC CARD from your LUNCHBOX. Now go to 18.

They were still looking for where the railway line came out again when George spotted a large heap of rocks. 'I wonder who could have put all those there?' she asked. Julian said that it was called a *cairn* and was built by local farmers in the old days to help people find their way. He then started to look for his map, thinking the cairn might show them how near they were to the tunnel's other end.

Use your MAP CARD to find out which square the cairn (heap of rocks) is in — then follow the instruction. If you don't have one, you'll have to guess which instruction to follow.

If you think D4	go to 42
If you think D3	go to 122
If you think E3	go to 85

On their way to the monument, Dick noticed there was a small statue at the top. He quickly called the others back, remembering something Jock's mother had told them. 'Perhaps this is the monument Mrs. Andrews was talking about,' he said excitedly, 'you remember, the one with a statue of Joshua Peters.' Joshua

Peters had been a famous tunnel builder in the area and Mrs. Andrews had described how the arm of his statue pointed towards one of his tunnels. They had thought the story rather charming at the time but now they realised it could be very useful as well! 'Before we get too excited, though,' said Anne, 'we had better check that we've got the right monument.' So they decided to look up Joshua Peters' monument on the map.

Use your MAP CARD to find out which square the monument with a statue is in – then follow the instruction. If you don't have one, you'll have to guess which instruction to follow.

If you think D3	go to 309
If you think E4	go to 189
If you think D4	go to 228

68

They followed their compass to a wide ledge about half-way up the cavern wall. On the ledge there were about half-a-dozen crates. Unfortunately, they were just too high up to see into but then George suggested that one of them should stand on another's shoulders. Since Anne was the lightest, she went at the top and since Julian was the strongest, he went at the bottom. 'Gosh, they're all full of valuable silverware!' exclaimed Anne. 'They must be worth a fortune.' *Go to 7.*

Timmy eagerly led the way, the rest following his black and white tail. Suddenly though, he stopped and pricked up his ears. 'What is it, Timmy?' the others asked anxiously, but then they heard something as well. It was three men talking further up the track – and not very pleasant men by the sound of it! One of them was saying that the lorry was to meet them at the level crossing. Certain the men were up to no good, The Five decided to look up the level crossing on the map in case they needed to tell the police about it later.

Use your MAP CARD to find out which square the level crossing is in – then follow the instruction. If you don't have one, you'll have to guess which instruction to follow.

If you think C4	go to 22
If you think D3	go to 6
If you think B3	go to 255

Suddenly, the train started to move! 'Oh, it *is* a ghost train, after all!' wailed Anne, nearly jumping out of her skin. But then they noticed that it was being driven by three rough-looking men. They crouched right down in the truck so the men wouldn't be able to see them. As soon as the train had gone through the arch, though, it stopped and the men came round. 'We'll leave it here ready,' one of them was saying – but then he noticed the top of George's head. 'What do you think you're doing here?' he asked angrily. 'Come to spy on us, have you?' Before The Five could escape, the men had seized them, forcing them back into the cavern. 'Well, you can just stay locked up in here until the operation's over!' they said. And, at that, the men left them there, closing the sliding wall again! **Go to 210.**

71

It was so dusty inside the tunnel that they soon decided to have some of their ginger beer. 'That's better!' said Anne, as she handed her bottle to Jock. He agreed, taking a long, delicious gulp.

Take one PICNIC CARD from your LUNCHBOX. Now go to 138.

72

But then Julian decided that it was much more important to try and find a way out first and so they left this clue for later. They went over to the sliding wall, trying to push it open again but it wouldn't budge. Exhausted, they sat down and had some of their picnic while they considered what to do next.

Take one PICNIC CARD from your LUNCHBOX. Now go to 221. (Remember: when there are no picnic cards left in your lunchbox, the game is over and you must start again.)

73

Dick's suggestion was to swing their lamp from side to side in the hope that someone at the farm might notice it and signal back. The idea worked! It wasn't long before another light started flashing in the distance. 'It's probably my mother, worried what's happened to me,' said Jock. Before they finished signalling, they decided to check the direction of the light with the compass. They would then know which way to go even if the flashing stopped.

Use your COMPASS CARD to work out the direction of the light by placing exactly over the shape below — and with pointer touching north. Then go to the number that appears in the window. If you don't have a COMPASS, you'll have to guess which number to go to.

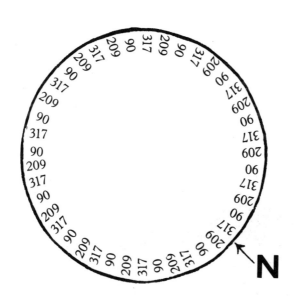

They had gone some way further when George suddenly stopped. She had noticed somebody's diary in the heather. 'Oh, do hurry up, George,' cried the others, 'or we're never going to make it.' George picked the diary up, though, glancing through the pages. It obviously belonged to one of the thieves because on one day's page there was a note about hiding silverware. Realising this could be vital evidence, George quickly turned to the front to find out the owner's name. But he had very cleverly written it in code! George called the others back, telling them to search for their codebooks.

Use your CODEBOOK CARD to find out this person's name by decoding the instruction below. If you don't have one, go to 103 instead.

They were sure they must be very near to the farm now, reaching a stone bridge. But, just to be certain, Julian suggested looking the bridge up on the map.

Use your MAP CARD to find out which square the bridge is in — then follow the instruction. If you don't have a MAP, you'll have to guess which instruction to follow.

<blockquote>

If you think B1 go to 12

If you think C1 go to 318

If you think B2 go to 116

</blockquote>

76

Dick's suggestion was to look for a light in the distance. Since Jock's house was the only building in the area, it was bound to be coming from there! When they searched round for a light, however, they could see nothing but darkness. 'Perhaps it's too far away,' said Anne. So they took off their rucksacks to look for their binoculars.

Use your BINOCULARS CARD to try and spot the light by placing exactly over the shape below — then follow the instruction. If you don't have one, go to 267 instead.

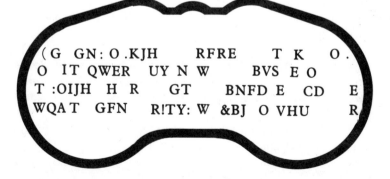

George insisted that she gave the directions, gabbling instructions to the driver as they went along the rough, bumpy track. When quite a time had passed, however, and they were still bumping along, the others began to worry that she had gone wrong somewhere. The track had just made a very sharp bend and so they decided to check it on the map.

Use your MAP CARD to find out which square the sharp bend is in – then follow the instruction there. If you don't have one, you'll have to guess which instruction to follow.

If you think B2	go to 130
If you think B3	go to 104
If you think C2	go to 57

78

Not long after, they arrived at a level crossing. They all jumped out of the van and then the driver took it further up the road to find a hiding place for it. 'The train is bound to wait here for the lorry,' said the sergeant, 'and so this is where we'll wait for the train!' He asked the children to look up the level crossing on the map so that he would know what direction to give if he had to radio back for extra help.

Use your MAP CARD to find out which square the level crossing is in – then follow the instruction. If you don't have one, you'll have to guess which instruction to follow.

If you think B4	go to 58
If you think D4	go to 199
If you think C4	go to 212

It was finally agreed they should follow Dick's idea and he led them into the next valley. 'If my calculations are right,' he said, half-way along, 'we should be able to see the railway line from the top of that ridge over there.' When they had climbed the ridge, however, they weren't sure whether they could see the railway line or not. There was something in the distance that *looked* a bit like one but perhaps it was just a farm track instead. It was far too far away to tell. Then Anne suddenly had an idea! 'Why don't we look through our binoculars?' she suggested.

Use your BINOCULARS CARD to find out whether it's the railway line or not by placing exactly over the shape below – then follow the instruction. If you don't have any BINOCULARS in your RUCKSACK, go to 213 instead.

G GN: O .KJH   RFRE   T K   O .
:LK T M.FR   NHRBW H: HGFR O N E
SIXTY(E VJHGFDS KMH! E RT G!A N
!AS N AZ!Q   BVHU I   DER N   XTR E

Even *with* the binoculars, however, they couldn't quite work out what it was. 'We'll just have to wait until we get a little nearer,' said Julian. Before they went a step further, though, George insisted that they have some of their picnic. Her tummy had been rumbling right through the mist! It was just as she was biting into a

slice of cherry cake that she suddenly realised what the shed was. 'It's a railway yard!' she exclaimed, spraying Timmy with crumbs. 'It must be the beginning of the line!'

Take one PICNIC CARD from your LUNCHBOX. Now go to 249.

81

They kept going, hoping that it wasn't much further now. Their legs were beginning to grow a little tired. The only one who didn't seem to care was Timmy. He looked as if he could quite happily trot along all day! *Continue to 38.*

82

By the time Anne had found her binoculars, though, Dick had stopped signalling. So they weren't sure whether he could see the tunnel's other end or not. 'Oh, he must be able to,' said Julian after a while, 'or he would have started coming back.' They therefore ran towards him, soon discovering that, yes, he could see it after all. In fact, it was right in front of them! But Dick had some less good news as well. He had been so eager to signal back that he forgot his signalling hand was still holding his lunchbox. It had come open and his bottle of ginger beer had fallen out.

Take one PICNIC CARD from your LUNCHBOX. Now go to 155. (Remember: when there are no picnic cards left in your lunchbox, the game is over and you must start again.)

83

Timmy stood panting at the monument's fence, waiting for the others to catch him up. 'Oh, you always win, Timmy!' they yelled as they came up to it as well. 'We can't possibly run as fast as you.' When they had got their breath back, they started scanning round for the tunnel. 'I can't see the other end anywhere,' said Dick, shielding his eyes with his hand. Nor could the others. They were just wondering what to next when Anne noticed a small inscription carved into the monument's stone. They stepped over the fence to have a closer look, finding that it was in some sort of code. 'A good job we have codebooks with us!' declared George.

Use your CODEBOOK CARD to find out what this

inscription said by decoding the instruction below. If you don't have one, go to 43 instead.

84

George led them up, puffing and panting until she had reached the top of the track. There was a fine view over the nearby hills but where the railway line came out again was nowhere to be seen. It must have been hidden in a dip somewhere. They had a guess as to which direction it might be but they hadn't walked far when Timmy sniffed out a very deep hole. 'It's an air vent for the tunnel,' said George, squeezing her head in, 'and look – there's some writing on one of the bricks!' The only trouble was – it was in some sort of code!

*Use your **CODEBOOK CARD** to find out what this writing said by decoding the instruction below. If you don't have one, go to 152 instead.*

85

'Look, it's not far away at all!' said Julian, pointing to where the railway started again at the edge of the map. All they had to do was walk straight ahead for a few hundred yards. But as you can guess, they didn't walk at all. They *ran* as fast as they could. **Go to 155.**

Just at that very moment, though, they suddenly heard a voice from behind. It echoed so much that they couldn't work out who it was. All except for Timmy, that is, who started barking back in reply. But it wasn't a fierce bark. It was one of his friendly ones instead! 'Why, it's Jock!' Anne suddenly realised when they heard the voice again. Jock soon caught them up, explaining that his stepfather had gone out for the rest of the day and so he had come to join them. They were so pleased to see him that they all celebrated with a piece of his mother's cake.

Take one PICNIC CARD from your LUNCHBOX. Now go to 47.

By the time they had taken their binoculars out, however, the figures had moved further up the track. They decided they would just have to run after them. As they caught them up a bit, they could see that they were three unpleasant-looking men. Suddenly, Anne started to hiccup! 'Ssh!' whispered the others, 'or they'll hear us.' Her hiccups only became louder, though, and so they paused while she had a quick drink.

Take one PICNIC CARD from your LUNCHBOX. Now go to 113.

'What do you think you're doing here?' the men asked them roughly. 'Come to spy on us, have you?' But, before they could answer, the men had grabbed hold of them. 'Well, we'll just have to make sure you stay here until the operation's over,' they said, beginning to tie them up. The men then left them there, closing the sliding wall again so they couldn't escape. 'Oh, these knots are impossible,' said Dick as he tried to loosen them, but then he suddenly remembered Timmy. He could bite through them with his sharp teeth! As soon as their hands were free again, they went to investigate the trucks. They were full of large crates containing valuable silverware. 'Hey, look!' said Dick, 'this crate has got a coded message scribbled on the side.' They eagerly searched for their codebooks.

*Use your **CODEBOOK CARD** to find out what this message said by decoding the instruction below. If you don't have one, go to 72 instead.*

It was decided Timmy should climb the shaft first so the others could help push him up. Being a dog, he couldn't grip the rungs as easily as they could. They had been climbing for a good ten minutes when their lamp lit up a message painted on to the brick. 'Blow, it's in code!' said Julian, 'we'll need to get out our codebooks.' So they each asked the one behind to look through their rucksacks for them. Poor old Dick, at the bottom, didn't have anyone to search his!

*Use your **CODEBOOK CARD** to find out what this message said by decoding the instruction below. If you don't have one, go to 257 instead.*

They hadn't been following their compasses far when their lamp lit up a small book in the heather. George sent Timmy to pick it up so they wouldn't waste any time stopping. 'Why, it's a codebook!' she exclaimed as Timmy pushed it into her hand. Just in case it contained different codes to their books, they took it with them.

If you don't already have it, put the CODEBOOK CARD into your RUCKSACK. Go to 162.

They had walked quite a way further when they saw a farm truck ahead. 'That's Jim, one of our labourers!' said Jock. They all shouted after him, begging him to stop, but Jim couldn't hear them. He had soon disappeared into the darkness. Just before he did, though, Dick took note of which direction he was going so they could look it up on the compass. That way, they should be able to follow the short cut themselves!

Use your COMPASS CARD to work out this direction by placing exactly over the shape below — and with pointer touching north. Then go to the number that appears in the window. If you don't have a COMPASS, you'll have to guess which number to go to.

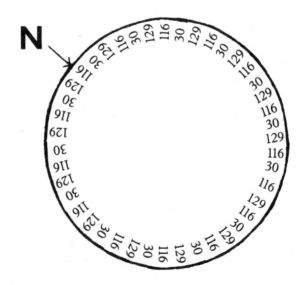

92

A sudden wind blew up, however, and they found it impossible to keep their maps open. 'Mine's blowing all over the place!' cried Dick as it wrapped round his face. They decided they would just have to guess which branch of the track to take, choosing the one to the right. On their way, they dropped some of their sandwiches for the birds to make their lunchboxes lighter.

Take one PICNIC CARD from your LUNCHBOX. Now go to 74.

93

Soon after they met the railway, they all jumped out while the driver went to hide the van on the other side of the crossing. 'The train is bound to wait here for the lorry,' said the sergeant, 'and so this is where we'll wait for the train!' The Five started looking for their binoculars so they would have a good view of when the train was coming.

*Use your **BINOCULARS CARD** to watch for the train by placing exactly on the shape below – then follow the instruction. If you don't have one, go to 32 instead.*

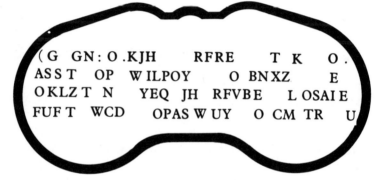

94

'We should have offered that shepherd some of our picnic,' said Anne, as they were glad to be taking the lower ground again. 'Never mind,' said Dick. 'Perhaps we'll meet him again on the way back.' *Go to 2.*

95

'Those boulders would make a great place to shelter if it rained,' said Dick as they continued on their journey. 'As long as that top one doesn't suddenly over-balance!' chuckled the others. Even Timmy seemed to join in the joke, his mouth making a great big grin! *Go to 304.*

The mist had become so thick, however, that the compass was impossible to read. 'I hope this doesn't become any heavier,' said Anne, 'or we won't even be able to see the end of our noses.' Then they all started laughing as they thought of poor Timmy. It was even worse for him. His nose was much further away than theirs! ***Go to 36.***

'I wonder what this line was for?' George asked as they continued along the stones in the middle. It was hard to imagine that it was to carry passengers in a place as deserted as this. 'It was probably to transport clay,' said Julian. 'There are quite a lot of clay-pits near here.'

Continue with them along the track to 186.

They had only walked a short way from the monument when they came across some wild ponies grazing amongst the heather. 'Oh, aren't they lovely!' said Anne, stroking their long, shaggy manes. George thought it would be fun to try and ride one of them, choosing the smallest. But as she climbed on to its back, it suddenly started, making her roll off. 'That serves you right!' the others all chuckled as she rubbed her elbows. ***Go to 4.***

99

The map showed several mires in this area, however, and they weren't sure which one it was! Knowing how dangerous a mire could be, they thought it best to return up the hill. All this extra climbing was making them so hot that they decided to have some of their ginger beer. 'Just the thing!' said Dick happily, as the bubbles fizzed up his nose.

Take one PICNIC CARD from your LUNCHBOX. Now go to 18.

100

'How are we going to get out?' asked George anxiously but then she suddenly realised that the men hadn't noticed Timmy. With his sharp teeth, he could bite through their ropes! As soon as they were untied, Dick went to pick up a scrap of paper from the floor. He had seen it drop from one of the men's pockets before he left. *'WE'LL MEET AT THE SHEPHERD'S HUT,'* it read, *'THEN START THE OPERATION AT MIDNIGHT.'* The Five started to look for their maps to see where the shepherd's hut was.

Use your MAP CARD to find out which square the shepherd's hut is in – then follow the instruction. If you don't have one, you'll have to guess which instruction to follow.

If you think D3   go to 72
If you think B3   go to 243
If you think C3   go to 207

Julian held the lamp in front of him as he led the way. After about a hundred yards or so, however, the branch-line suddenly ended. It looked as if it had once continued through a large arch in the wall but that arch was now bricked-up. They were just about to turn back again when Anne noticed a message chalked on to the tunnel roof. Julian lifted the lamp as high as he could so that they could read it. *'FOR SECRET LEVER,'* it said, *'WALK EIGHT PACES DUE EAST.'* Jock helped them look for their compasses.

Use your COMPASS CARD to find this lever by placing exactly over the shape below — and with pointer touching north. Then go to the number that appears in the window. If you don't have a COMPASS, you'll have to guess which number to go to.

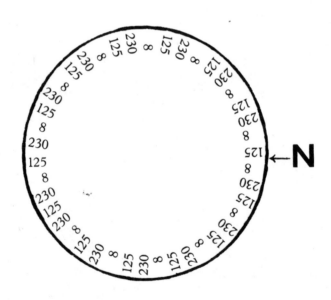

They returned to the sliding wall, attempting to open it again. They tried a lot harder this time but it was just as hopeless as

before. So they desperately searched round for any other way out. Maybe a secret door or passage! Finally, they found part of the wall that sounded hollow. Knocking it again, they were surprised to see a small section of the rock swing back on a hinge. 'There *is* a secret door!' cried Dick as they all crawled through. On the other side of the door was a long, vertical shaft with iron rungs leading all the way up. 'It must be an air vent!' said Julian as they prepared for the difficult climb.

Throw the FAMOUS FIVE dice to decide who is to go up the rungs first.

JULIAN thrown	go to 231
DICK thrown	go to 208
GEORGE thrown	go to 56
TIMMY thrown	go to 89
ANNE thrown	go to 144
MYSTERY thrown	go to 277

103

Unfortunately, the person had used a different code to the one in their books and so they couldn't find out his name after all. 'We're just going to have to make sure we catch them in the act,' said Julian, hurriedly starting off again. It was only some time later that Anne realised she had lost her map. She must have left it on the ground while searching for her codebook.

If you have one, take the MAP CARD from your RUCKSACK. Now go to 116.

104

The map showed that they *were* on the right road and so George knew what she was doing after all. 'Well done, lad!' said the sergeant, patting her on the back. It made the others secretly chuckle but George, of course, was quite delighted by the mistake! ***Go to 93.***

It was agreed that Dick should sit in the front and he directed the way along the rough, bumpy track. Suddenly, though, he could no longer recognise the route and he became worried that they had taken a wrong turning. 'If only we had a pair of binoculars,' said the sergeant, 'then we could check whether the tunnel is ahead or not.' The next thing he knew, The Five were hurriedly searching through their rucksacks!

*Use your **BINOCULARS CARD** to try and spot the tunnel by placing exactly on the shape below – then follow the instruction. If you don't have one, go to 224 instead.*

(G GN : O .KJH   RFRE   T K   O .
M.F T LOU!   ?JNM W K   YTR! O E
T WAS?   H RIKLOP   J.MNH(/ E   OPX E
RTF F ZTB   WQA O   WV U   SAPO R

They all agreed that Julian should take the lead himself and they held on to the back of his anorak as he moved slowly forward. 'I hope we don't walk into any mires,' said George anxiously, knowing how common they were in this area. Fortunately, though, the mist soon lifted and they were able to see where they were going again. They hadn't gone much further before Anne spotted a cigarette packet in the grass. 'Fancy spoiling the countryside like that!' she exclaimed, picking it up. She was just about to put it in her pocket when she noticed a coded message on the other side. 'I wonder if it has something to do with the railway line?' asked Dick excitedly as they all looked for their codebooks.

Use your CODEBOOK CARD to find out what this message said by decoding the instruction below. If you don't have a CODEBOOK in your RUCKSACK, go to 202 instead.

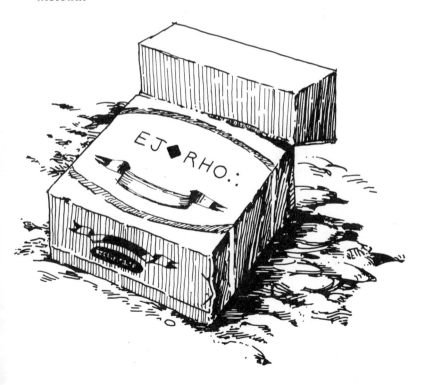

Since taking this path was really Dick's idea, it was agreed that he should be the one to go first. But it didn't lead to the railway after all, just another bleak valley. Moments later, though, Timmy noticed a welcome sight coming the other way. It was a family of pony-riders. 'Oh, aren't they lucky!' exclaimed Anne, wishing that she could have a holiday like that. Julian shouted *hello* to them, asking if they knew the way to the railway line. 'Go south-east from here,' the father shouted back with a friendly wave. It wasn't until the family was some way past, however, that Julian realised they could only follow their direction with the help of a compass.

Use your COMPASS CARD to find the way by placing exactly over the shape below – and with pointer touching north. Then go to the number that appears in the window. If you don't have a COMPASS in your RUCKSACK, you'll have to guess which number to go to.

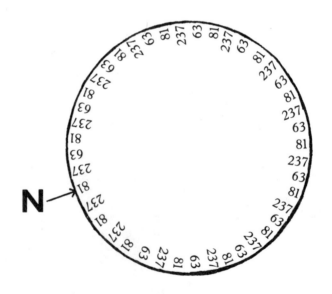

108

'I hope this mist doesn't stay all day,' said Dick as they at last started moving again. So did the others. Not only wouldn't they be able to find the railway line but they wouldn't be able to find their way back again either! Then they remembered Timmy. Of course ... he could sniff out the route they had come by. Now the mist didn't seem quite such a worry after all! *Go to 36.*

109

On reaching the monument, George had a quick walk round it. 'Look, I've found a small door at the back,' she told the others when they caught her up. Pushing the door open, they discovered there was a narrow staircase leading all the way to the top. They began to climb it, twisting round and round until they stepped out on to a high platform protected by railings. Spotting the tunnel's other end was now quite easy! So they would be able to remember which direction it was when they reached the bottom again, Dick suggested checking it on a compass.

Use your COMPASS CARD to find the tunnel's direction by placing exactly over the shape below – and with

*pointer touching north. **Then go to the number that
appears in the window. If you don't have a COMPASS,
you'll have to guess which number to go to.***

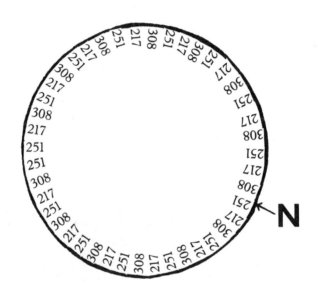

110
The writing on the bricks said that the other end of the tunnel was
another half mile along. 'It's a pity it didn't say which direction it
was as well,' remarked Anne. Still, at least they now knew that it
wasn't far! ***Go to 66.***

111
The tunnel's other end was very soon only a short distance ahead
and they hurried towards it. On the way, though, Anne tripped
over a small rock and dropped her lunchbox. Her cake crumbled
into such small pieces that she decided just to throw them away for

the birds. There was one piece the birds didn't receive, however. It was a big cherry – and Timmy went after that instead!

*Take one **PICNIC CARD** from your **LUNCHBOX**. Now go to 155.* (Remember: when there are no picnic cards left in your rucksack, the game is over and you must start again.)

112

The scrap of paper was addressed to someone called Bill and said: *'DON'T WORRY ABOUT WOODEN-LEG SAM. HE THINKS IT'S JUST A GHOST TRAIN!'* 'This whole business is becoming more and more mysterious!' said Julian, as they continued on their way. *Continue with them to 138.*

113

The men stopped for a cigarette where the branch-line suddenly ended. It looked as if it had once continued through a large arch in the wall but that arch was now bricked-up. Next, though, something amazing happened. One of the men pulled a lever in the wall and the whole of the bricked-up part slowly began to open! The Five gasped at what they saw on the other side. It was a huge cavern and, right in the middle, stood an old steam train and a couple of trucks! When the men weren't looking, The Five crept into the cavern as well but then one man suddenly turned round and spotted them. *Go to 88.*

114

George's suggestion was such a good one that they decided to try hers. It was that Timmy should bark as loudly as he could to attract the sheep dogs on Jock's farm. They then might bark back in reply and The Five could follow the sound. The idea worked! On Timmy's third bark, one came back from the distance. 'That's Shep!' cried Jock excitedly. 'I'd recognise her bark anywhere.' So The Five started on their way, Timmy adding another bark every hundred yards or so. They had gone quite a distance when Julian trod on something hard amongst the heather. It was a gun with a broken trigger. 'It must have been thrown away by one of the thieves!' Julian said excitedly. Looking closer, he noticed there was an inscription on it. *'THIS IS THE PROPERTY OF . . .'* it began but the person's name was in code. They all started looking for their codebooks.

Use your CODEBOOK CARD to find out who the owner was by decoding the instruction below. If you don't have one, go to 196 instead.

115

'We need to go in the direction of that stream over there,' said Julian when they had found the shepherd's hut on the map. Fortunately, the moon had come out a little and the stream showed up nice and brightly. **Go to 91.**

116

Finally having reached the farm, they ran inside to tell Jock's step-father what they had discovered. They could only find his mother, though, who had been very worried about them. She said that Mr. Andrews was still in town and so they had better ring the police themselves. After a long, anxious wait, the police finally arrived. The sergeant said that they had been after this gang of silver thieves for a long time and it was essential that they didn't get away. So they took The Famous Five with them in their van to show them where the tunnel was.

Throw the FAMOUS FIVE DICE to decide who is to sit in the front and direct the police.

JULIAN thrown	go to 34
DICK thrown	go to 105
GEORGE thrown	go to 77
ANNE thrown	go to 198
TIMMY thrown	go to 181
MYSTERY thrown	go to 259

117

When they reached the bridge, they decided to have a quick rest. They were just about to set off again when Anne noticed an old biscuit tin hidden under the bridge's arch. Being careful not to slip into the water, she went to have a closer look at it. It sounded as if there was something inside and so she opened the lid. 'Look, it's some sort of codebook!' she called to the others on the bank. They took it with them in case it might have some use later on. You never knew in a place like this!

If you don't already have it, put the CODEBOOK CARD into your RUCKSACK. Now go to 14.

118

They had only turned the next bend when George spotted something else. This time she was even more excited. 'Look, it's where the railway starts!' she said, pointing to a large yard immediatcly in front of them. The adventure was now really about to begin . . .! *Go to 249.*

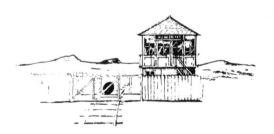

119

Timmy seemed the obvious choice and they all followed his tail as he sniffed his way forward. It was a good job his tail had a white patch on the end! They hadn't gone far like this when they heard a small whine from him. 'Oh, what is it, Timmy?' cried George, thinking he might have broken his leg or something. But it wasn't as serious as that. He had merely bumped his nose on something sticking up from the ground. They all gathered round to see what it was. 'Hooray, it's a sign!' cried Dick but, as they looked closer, they noticed that it was in some sort of code. They quickly took off their rucksacks to look for a codebook.

Use your CODEBOOK CARD to find out what the sign said by decoding the instruction below. If you don't have a CODEBOOK in your RUCKSACK, go to 201 instead.

EJIRHA

120

Julian waited for the others to reach the monument, then they all searched for where the railway came out again. But it was nowhere to be seen. 'It must be hidden behind a ridge somewhere,' said

Dick. They were just about to leave the monument when George noticed there was an inscription on it. It read, *'THIS IS TO THE MEMORY OF JOSHUA PETERS, A FAMOUS TUNNEL-BUILDER OF THE AREA. ONE OF HIS TUNNEL LIES HALF A MILE DUE EAST FROM HERE.'* Unable to believe their luck, they searched for their compasses.

Use your COMPASS CARD to find the right direction by placing exactly over the shape below — and with pointer touching north. Then go to the number that appears in the window. If you don't have a COMPASS, you'll have to guess which number to go to.

121

They hadn't followed Dick's compass far when it suddenly slipped from his hand. They all chased after it as it began to roll down the hill. Finally, they managed to stop it - but not before making themselves a long walk up again! *Go to 18.*

122

When Julian studied his map, however, he saw that the other end of the tunnel wasn't shown. It must have been just off the map's edge. 'What a pity,' said Julian . . . but the very next moment they spotted it. The tunnel exit had been right beneath them all the time! They were in such a hurry to scramble down to it that Anne dropped her lunchbox. The lid sprang open from the jolt, some of her sandwiches spilling on to the ground. They were so dirty that they just had to be left for the birds.

Take one PICNIC CARD from your LUNCHBOX before continuing to 155. (Remember: When there are no picnic cards left in your lunchbox, the game is over and you must start again.)

123

The other end was obviously too far off even for the binoculars, though, and so they put them away again. They were just about to agree that there wasn't going to be enough light to continue when the tunnel suddenly lit up! Someone was coming after them with a lamp. To begin with, they couldn't work out who it was but then they realised. 'Why, it's Jock!' they all shouted with joy, 'what are you doing here?' He explained that his stepfather had gone out for the rest of the day and he had come to join their adventure. So not only did The Five now have a lamp, they also had someone to help them! ***Go to 47.***

The message became much bigger through their binoculars and they could now read all of it. *'TO OPEN THE WALL FROM THE INSIDE OF THE CAVERN,'* it said, *'PRESS THE MIDDLE BRICK THREE ROWS UP FROM THE BOTTOM.'* They hurriedly found this brick but, as hard as they pressed, they couldn't make it work. 'The men must have switched the mechanism off,' Julian said as they all sat despondently against the train. **Go to 221.**

They were still looking for their compasses when Dick suddenly realised they didn't need one. The message had an arrow chalked next to it, showing which way east was! Having measured the eight paces, they felt around the tunnel wall. Their fingers suddenly touched a long iron bar, hidden in a groove. They pulled the lever down and, slowly, the bricked-up part began to move! Anne was so amazed by it that she dropped her lunchbox, breaking her bottle of ginger beer.

Take one PICNIC CARD from your LUNCHBOX. Now go to 140.

'It's just a sheet of paper,' said Anne with relief as she focused her binoculars, 'it seems to have been caught on a ledge.' When she had climbed up to it, however, she saw that it wasn't caught at all. Someone had put a stone on top of it to stop it blowing away. Nor was it just a sheet of paper. It was a map of the moors! Since it looked more detailed than their own, they decided to take it with them.

If you don't already have it, put the MAP CARD into your RUCKSACK. Now go to 160.

127

Then Jock suddenly had an idea himself. The bedroom window from which he could just see the tunnel faced south. To get from the tunnel back to the house, therefore, they simply had to go north! A second later, they were all quickly searching for their compasses.

Use your COMPASS CARD to find this direction by placing exactly over the shape below — and with pointer touching north. Then go to the number that appears in the window. If you don't have a COMPASS, you'll have to guess which number to go to.

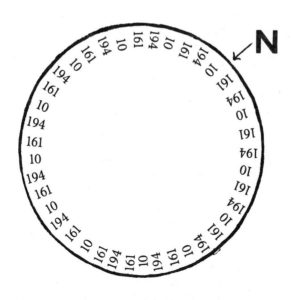

'Yes, there *is* a waterfall!' cried Anne as she looked through her binoculars. So they quickly set off in the lake's direction, thankful that there was a bright moon. ***Go to 75.***

'The truck was going east,' said Dick excitedly as they started to run in the direction his compass indicated. They hadn't been running for long, however, before Jock tripped on something amongst the heather. He sprained his ankle slightly and Julian went to find out what had caused it while Jock had a short rest. 'It's a pair of binoculars!' he exclaimed, giving them to Jock to make him feel better.

If you don't already have it, put the BINOCULARS CARD into your RUCKSACK. Now go to 116.

But the track was so bumpy that the maps were impossible to read. Julian suggested that they should stop but the sergeant said it would waste too much time and they would just have to hope for the best. If this *wasn't* the right way, he added, they would probably be too late anyway! ***Go to 93.***

Finally deciding it would be safer if Timmy went first, they all followed him along the side of the hill. 'Timmy makes the best guide anywhere!' George said proudly to the others. He led them carefully down to where the path ended at a small brook below. 'Phew! Thank goodness that's over!' said Dick. Now that they were on low ground again, Timmy started to run excitedly ahead. He seemed to think that the railway was round any corner now. 'Not too fast!' shouted the others, unable to keep up. Timmy had already disappeared over the next brow, however, and by the time they reached it themselves he was too small to see. 'Which direction did he go?' they all asked in bewilderment. The only way they were going to find out was with a pair of binoculars.

*Use your **BINOCULARS CARD** to track Timmy down by placing exactly over the shape below – then follow the instruction. If you don't have any **BINOCULARS** in your **RUCKSACK**, go to 37 instead.*

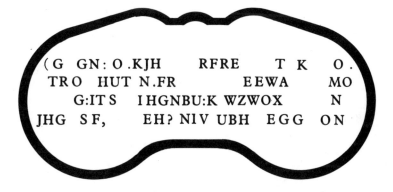

(G GN: O .KJH   RFRE   T K   O .
TRO HUT N.FR   EEWA   MO
   G:ITS   I HGNBU:K WZWOX   N
JHG S F,   EH? NIV UBH EGG ON

132

On climbing the next slope, they spotted an old man sitting amongst the heather. They couldn't understand it. 'How peculiar – sitting in the middle of nowhere like that!' remarked Anne as they went over to him. As they got nearer, however, they noticed that he had a drawing board on his lap. Of course, that explained it – he was an artist painting the moors! 'Hello,' they greeted him, peering over his shoulder, 'do you mind if we have a look?' The artist didn't mind at all, glad of someone's interest. 'Gosh, it's beautiful!' they all exclaimed, amazed how real it looked. They then asked him if he could help direct them to the old railway line. 'Certainly, children,' the old man replied, 'you need to go south from here. You all have compasses with you, I trust?'

Use your COMPASS CARD to find the right direction by placing exactly over the shape below — and with pointer touching north. Then go to the number that appears in the window. If you don't have a COMPASS in your RUCKSACK, you'll have to guess which number to go to.

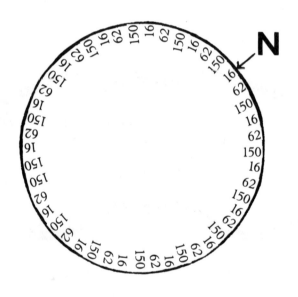

Just at that moment, a strange thing happened! The mist suddenly thinned, revealing a circle of stones ahead. But, seconds later, the mist closed in again and the stones were gone. They wondered what the circle was, turning to Julian for an answer. 'They were built in the Stone Age,' he informed them, 'and are quite common in this area.' He then thought of looking it up on his map as a rough guide to where they were.

Use your MAP CARD to find out which square the circle of stones is in – then follow the instruction. If you don't have a MAP in your RUCKSACK, you'll have to guess which number to go to.

If you think A2	go to 36
If you think B2	go to 215
If you think C2	go to 108

134
The winner of the race was Anne and they all leant over her shoulder as she decoded the secret message. It said that the train was to come out as far as the level crossing. 'I wonder what that means?' asked Dick as they continued on their way. What intrigued them even more, though, was that the message looked fairly recent! *Go to 172.*

135
They decided looking for their binoculars would waste too much time, though, and it would be better to hurry to the top of the hill themselves. If there was someone up there, they might just be able to catch them. When they reached the top, however, there was not a soul in sight! But then Timmy started to sniff after someone's scent. The others all followed him towards a distant ridge and down the other side. Suddenly there in front of them was a sheep, innocently grazing on the slope! 'So that's who dislodged the rock!' they all laughed. They were so relieved that they decided to

sit down and have some of their picnic before returning to the top of the hill.

Take one PICNIC CARD from your LUNCHBOX. Now go to 18.

136

Just before leaving the monument, they thought it would be a good idea to check the direction they had to go on the compass. That way, they would always have something to guide them by. So they played 'Potato' to see who had to take their compass out. The loser was Dick!

Use your COMPASS CARD to check the direction they needed to walk by placing exactly over the shape below – and with pointer touching north. Then go to the number that appears in the window. If you don't have a COMPASS, you'll have to guess which number to go to.

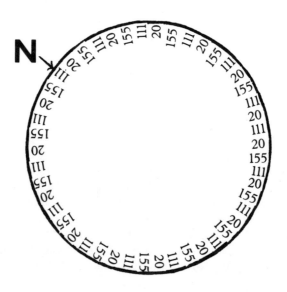

Julian was left with the shortest blade of grass himself and so he nervously led the way into the tunnel. It became more and more difficult to see as the entrance became smaller and smaller behind them. 'How stupid we were not to bring a torch,' Julian said, 'we're never going to find any clues in this dark.' They had only gone a few yards further when they suddenly heard a noise from behind. 'W-w-what is it?' asked Anne, not daring to look round. Finally, they did have the courage to look round, seeing a dark figure right back at the entrance. But he was so far away, they couldn't really tell what he was up to. Dick then had the idea of using their binoculars.

Use your BINOCULARS CARD to obtain a better look at this figure by placing exactly over the shape below – then follow the instruction. If you don't have any BINO-CULARS, go to 253 instead.

```
( G  GN: O .KJH        RFRE        T  K      O
TYUO  WJAS      HQOPN D  E   D  Y  Q     R  J
I S      ZAM E  V ASDILPOY?  X   WE  CVB   ON
  ZAS F     MBO  YUIO      V IUY U  BVCE      R R
```

They hadn't gone much further along the tunnel when part of the line suddenly branched off to the left. And, when they brought their lamp nearer, they noticed it was a lot shinier than the rest! 'This branch has obviously been used fairly recently,' said Dick excitedly. They decided to follow it, holding the lamp high above their heads. It wasn't long, though, before the branch suddenly ended. It looked as if it had once continued through a large arch in the tunnel wall but that arch was now bricked-up. A moment later, something extraordinary happened ... Timmy rested his paw against one of the bricks and the arch slowly began to open! *Go to 313.*

139

'It's three men,' said Julian as they focused their binoculars, '– and pretty mean men, by the look of it!' They began to follow them to see what they were up to. They were sure it couldn't be any good! *Go to 113.*

140

The bricked-up part opened wider and wider, finally revealing a large cavern on the other side. And in the middle of the cavern was an old steam train with a couple of trucks! 'Here's our ghost train!' said Julian, as they rushed in to have a better look. There was nothing ghostly about the train at all, though. It was perfectly real! 'Hey, look at these,' called Dick, investigating some boxes in one of the trucks, 'they're full of valuable silverware!' Just as the others came over, though, they suddenly heard a rough-sounding voice from behind. *Go to 310.*

'Yes, it *is* our farmhouse!' Jock cried as he focused the binoculars Anne had lent him. 'I can now see the chimneys. There are two big ones and one short one.' As they were running towards it, Timmy suddenly dropped behind. The others were just beginning to worry about him, when he caught them up again, carrying something in his mouth. 'Look, it's a codebook' exclaimed George, '– and I wouldn't mind betting it belongs to one of those thieves!' Just in case it did, they decided to take it along to the police so they could check it for finger prints.

If you don't already have it, put the CODEBOOK CARD into your RUCKSACK. Now go to 116.

Suddenly, there was a strong gust of wind and it snatched the plan right out of Dick's hand! They tried chasing it for a while but the wind blew it further and further away. 'Now we'll never know whose signature it was,' said Dick disappointedly. The chase had made them so hot that they had a quick drink of their ginger beer before continuing.

Take one PICNIC CARD from your LUNCHBOX. Now go to 75.

Timmy couldn't tell them his suggestion, of course, but he obviously had one because he suddenly set off down the hill! 'I wonder what he's up to?' asked the others as they chased after him. Then they realised. He had probably picked up their scent from the journey there and was following it back again! After quite a while, though, he stopped as if he had lost it. The children tried to help him, seeing if they could remember anything. 'Yes, those large boulders over there!' Dick cried suddenly. 'On the way, we turned south-west at them and so now we must go north-east.' They quickly searched for their compasses.

*Use your **COMPASS CARD** to find this direction by placing exactly over the shape below — and with pointer touching north. Then go to the number that appears in the window. If you don't have a **COMPASS**, you'll have to guess which number to go to.*

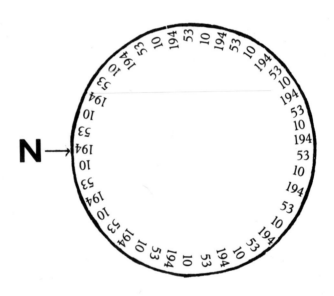

144

Anne led the way, having decided that first was probably much better than last! Suddenly though, she heard a strange flapping noise from above. 'Ooh, what is it?' she cried, thinking it might be an owl. They all looked up into the darkness above, seeing a white shape. But it was too far away to work out what it was. 'Let's use our binoculars,' whispered Dick. So they all quietly looked through their rucksacks.

Use your BINOCULARS CARD to see what this shape was by placing exactly over the shape below. Then follow the instruction. If you don't have any BINOCULARS, go to 244 instead.

(G GN: O .KJH   RFRE   T K   O .
T W   MKJ:O MNB   N L   KJHG: E CD
  BJ FDS T   EIUR   VIJH TRE W   N O
  TF S HGFD   B (LW I LOU   X

Just before the lorry-driver became visible, however, he realised it was a trap and quickly turned his lorry round. By the time the police had fetched their van again, he had disappeared into the darkness. 'Well, he got away this time,' sighed the sergeant, 'but he's bound to be back to try and rescue the rest of that loot.' And when he does come back, thought The Five, they would be there to help foil him!

Your adventure wasn't quite successful. If you would like another attempt at solving the mystery, you must start again at paragraph one.

Finally deciding on Anne's idea, they all followed her towards a rough farm track that led into the distance. They hadn't gone far along the track, however, before it suddenly started to rain. 'Quick, what shall we do?' asked Dick as their anoraks became more and more soaked. There seemed absolutely nowhere to take cover – not a tree in sight! Then Julian spotted what looked like an old sheep shelter some distance to their left. 'Are you sure it's a sheep shelter?' asked George. 'We don't want to go all that way if it's just a large rock.' They all began to squint at it to try and make out what it was but then Dick had a better idea! They could use a pair of binoculars instead.

Use your BINOCULARS CARD to find out whether it's a shelter or not by placing exactly over the shape below — then follow the instruction. If you don't have any BINOCULARS in your RUCKSACK, go to 183 instead.

```
( G  GN : O .KJH      RFRE      T  K     O .
TUB     FRT( T HGJ(? W R  O QWE H    RE
: EV.C      I G BNJ? JM:LKF      H !A?& :K T
!GJS  U:,HG  E  NH:,J V  NBUIE  J.MNE  N
```

The message did have something to do with the railway line! *'TRAIN WILL RUN AT TWO IN THE MORNING'* it said, once they had decoded it. Then Jock was right – it did still operate. But they wondered who had written the message and why.

Hopefully, they would soon have some answers! *Go to 132.*

148

The message said that the beginning of the railway line was exactly half a mile further on. 'But it doesn't say which direction,' objected George, looking round. Then she spotted a number of rusting sheds in the distance. 'It's a railway yard!' she shouted, suddenly recognising what it was. They all hurried towards it but stopped for a moment on the way when Anne noticed something shining in the grass. It was a compass! They quickly popped it into one of their rucksacks before continuing.

If you don't already have it, put the COMPASS CARD into your RUCKSACK. Now go to 249.

'Not a soul in sight!' said Julian, scanning right to the path's end. Just as he was about to put the binoculars away again, however, he spotted a small object lying a short distance ahead. When they reached the exact point, they saw that it was a compass – obviously dropped by someone. 'We'd probably never have noticed it without the binoculars,' remarked George as they took the compass with them in case they needed a spare.

If you don't already have it, put the COMPASS CARD into your RUCKSACK. Now go to 38.

'Yes, we have a compass each,' Julian answered, 'they're in our rucksacks.' The artist gave an approving nod of his head. 'Very wise, very wise,' he said, 'it would be highly dangerous to come on the moors without one.' ***Go to 62.***

'It must be miles,' exclaimed George, 'I can't even see it *with* the binoculars!' Then she had a look through the binoculars at Timmy. Why, even *he* seemed to be miles away – and yet he was standing right next to her! 'It's because you've got them the wrong way round!' laughed Julian, with the others joining in. George went into such a mood that it was a quarter of an hour before she would talk to them again. ***Go to 186.***

In trying to read the writing in the hole, however, George leant in so far that she overturned! The others were only just able to grab her legs in time. Otherwise, she might well have fallen all the way to the bottom. Since it was so dangerous, they decided they would just have to forget about decoding the message. Instead, they would have some of their picnic!

Take one PICNIC CARD from your LUNCHBOX. Now go to 66.

153

Dick's compass pointed them towards a narrow valley below and they all hurried down to it. Instead of coming to the railway line, though, they arrived at a large mire! 'This can't be right,' said Dick – and then he realised what had happened. The pointer of his compass had become stuck! He then thought of looking up the mire on his map but it just wasn't Dick's day. A gust of wind tore it out of his hand and plopped it right in the middle of the mud! He daren't go after it in case he was sucked under. Sadly, he returned with the others up the hill.

If you have one, take the MAP CARD from your RUCKSACK. Now go to 18.

154

'I can't see the other end anywhere,' Dick called back when he had finally reached the top of the track. Nor could the others when they were standing there. 'The tunnel must run for miles,' said George, vainly searching for where the line came out again. All she could see was mile upon mile of purple hilltop. Then Anne had the obvious idea of using her binoculars. 'Of course, why didn't we think of that!' the others exclaimed as they searched for theirs as well.

Use your BINOCULARS CARD to try and spot the other

end of the tunnel by placing exactly over the shape below
– then follow the instruction. If you don't have one, go to
188 instead.

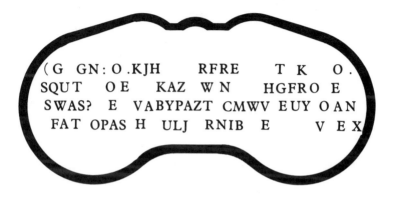

(G GN : O .KJH   RFRE   T K   O .
SQU T   O E   KAZ   W N   HGFRO E
 SWAS?   E   VABYPAZT CMWV EUY O AN
   FAT OPAS H   ULJ   RNIB   E   V E X

155

Arriving at the tunnel's other end, they all searched round for clues. But they couldn't find any. 'Well, we can't put it off any longer,' said Julian, 'we're just going to have to search the tunnel itself. If there *are* clues to be found, they're obviously going to be in there.' They walked up to the tunnel's dark, eerie mouth, hearing the slow drip, drip of water from inside. 'Who's going to go first?' Dick asked with a bit of a shiver. They thought the fairest thing to do was to draw straws for it. So Julian picked five blades of grass, hiding them behind his back.

Throw the FAMOUS FIVE DICE to decide who is to draw the shortest and enter the tunnel first.

JULIAN thrown	go to 137
DICK thrown	go to 219
GEORGE thrown	go to 190
ANNE thrown	go to 51
TIMMY thrown	go to 24
MYSTERY thrown	go to 229

The coded message said that the goods were to be sent into town and sold on the secret market. The Five then turned their attentions to the sliding wall, seeing if they could push it open again but it wouldn't budge. 'Perhaps there's another lever on the inside,' said Dick hopefully as they started looking round for it. Unfortunately, they didn't find one but they *did* find a compass! It must have been dropped by one of the men.

If you don't already have it, put the COMPASS CARD into your RUCKSACK. Now go to 221.

Their compasses pointed them towards the cavern wall but there were no crates to be found. 'Perhaps our compasses aren't working properly,' suggested Julian, 'the iron of the train might be distorting them.' So they decided to sit down instead and have a drink of their ginger beer. All the dust in there was making their throats dry. Just as Dick was pouring himself his second cupful, he noticed a small recess in the opposite wall. And packed inside were about half a dozen crates. 'Gosh, they're full of valuable silver-ware!' they said as they went over to investigate.

Take one PICNIC CARD from your LUNCHBOX. Now go to 7.

Leaping into the driver's cabin, Timmy just reached the train first. 'Well, that proves there's nothing ghostly about it!' exclaimed the others as they followed him in. They were examining the engine's controls when Anne noticed a log-book on the floor. It looked as if someone had tried to burn it in the furnace but it had fallen out again. Turning over the partly-charred pages, they discovered that one had a coded message on it. Before you could snap your fingers, they were looking for their codebooks!

*Use your **CODEBOOK CARD** to find out what this message said by decoding the instruction below. If you don't have one, go to 9 instead.*

George moved cautiously forward, the others sticking right behind. The branch-line didn't run for long, though, before it suddenly ended. It looked as if it had once continued through a large arch in the wall but that arch was now bricked-up. They thought it must have been done some time ago but then Jock noticed that some of the bricks looked quite new. The others started to examine the bricks too, Anne suddenly finding one with a message chiselled into it! When they brought their lamp nearer to the message, they saw that it was in some sort of code. Jock helped them look for their codebooks.

*Use your **CODEBOOK CARD** to find out what the message said by decoding the instruction below. If you don't have one, go to 8 instead.*

160

A few more rungs and they finally reached the top of the shaft, stepping out into the open air. It was now almost dark, however, making Julian rather concerned. 'We'd better hurry,' he said, 'or we're never going to reach the police station in time. The train will probably be driven out in an hour or two.' Jock said it would take much too long to go all the way to the police station and it would be better to ring them from his farm. It had become so difficult to see, though, that Jock wasn't sure which way to go. If Jock didn't know, then The Five were hardly likely to! But they all had a think, each coming up with a different suggestion.

Throw the FAMOUS FIVE DICE to decide whose suggestion to follow.

JULIAN thrown	go to 233
DICK thrown	go to 73
GEORGE thrown	go to 114
ANNE thrown	go to 197
TIMMY thrown	go to 285
MYSTERY thrown	go to 314

161

'I hope we're not going to be too late,' said Dick, when there still seemed a long way to go, 'or those men might get clean away.' If they *did* manage to catch them, on the other hand, there might even be a reward! *Go to 74.*

They had gone some way further when they spotted a shadowy building not too far ahead. Jock couldn't be sure whether it was his farmhouse or not. The others started looking for a pair of binoculars to help him work it out.

Use your BINOCULARS CARD to give Jock a clearer look at this building by placing exactly over the shape below – then follow the instruction. If you don't have one, go to 54 instead.

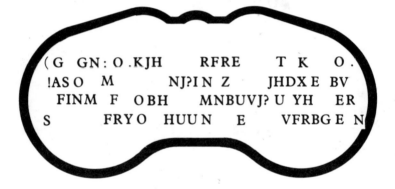

'Yes, it *is* one of our trucks,' cried Jock as Anne lent him her binoculars, 'I can just read the number plate!' So, remembering which direction it was going before it disappeared, they then started running the same way themselves. On the way, the light from their lamp made something gleam in the heather. It was a compass! They took it with them as a spare.

If you don't already have it, put the COMPASS CARD into your RUCKSACK. Now go to 75.

George had noticed the lights of a radio mast in the distance and her suggestion was to look it up on the map to see if it was in the same direction as the farm. If it was, then all they had to do was follow it. If it wasn't, then they would know they should go in another direction. So they all started looking for their maps.

Use your MAP CARD to find out which square the radio mast is in – then follow the instruction. If you don't have one, you'll have to guess which instruction to follow.

If you think A1	go to 180
If you think B1	go to 315
If you think C1	go to 286

Just as they were about to take their compasses out, however, Dick noticed two thin silver lines ahead. It was the railway, glistening in the moonlight! 'Oh, well done, Timmy,' George said, hugging him round the neck, 'you found the right way after all!' The others knew it was more by accident than by choice but they gave him a hug as well. When Anne gave him her hug she noticed that he was sitting on something. 'Look, it's a map!' she exclaimed. 'Timmy must have brought it from the farm in case we needed a spare!'

If you don't already have it, put the MAP CARD into your RUCKSACK. Now go to 78.

In the end, they all agreed on Julian's choice and he led them down the hill towards a small track at the bottom. At the track, he turned right. 'I'm sure Jock's window faced in *this* direction,' he said, walking briskly at the front. Half an hour later, however, and he was beginning to change his mind! There was nothing in the distance but a tall radio mast standing on a hill. They were just wondering what to do next when Dick suddenly had an idea. 'I know!' he said. 'We can look up the radio mast on the map to find out where we are.'

*Use your **MAP CARD** to find out which square the radio mast is in – then follow the instruction. If you don't have a **MAP** in your **RUCKSACK**, you'll have to guess which instruction to follow.*

If you think B1	go to 260
If you think C1	go to 292
If you think E1	go to 225

167

'There he is!' exclaimed Julian, pointing to the right. The others had a quick look through the binoculars as well before giving chase. 'Some guide!' commented Dick when they had finally caught him up. 'Yes, it's a funny guide that runs miles ahead,' Anne added. Timmy was instantly forgiven, however, when they saw that he had found a map amongst the heather. It was in quite good condition. 'See, I told them you were a good guide!' George smiled, hugging him round the neck.

*If you don't already have it, put the **MAP CARD** into your **RUCKSACK**. Now go to 2.*

It was finally agreed Anne should go first since she was the lightest should they suddenly have to grab hold of her. She felt her way slowly forward, hoping that they didn't come to a surprise drop! It wasn't until they had proceeded like this for a good quarter of a mile or so that Julian suddenly realised something. How did they know they weren't just going round and round in circles? To make sure, he looked for his compass.

Use your COMPASS CARD to find out which direction they're facing by placing exactly over the shape below — and with pointer touching north. Then go to the number that appears in the window. If you don't have a COMPASS in your RUCKSACK, you'll have to guess which number to go to.

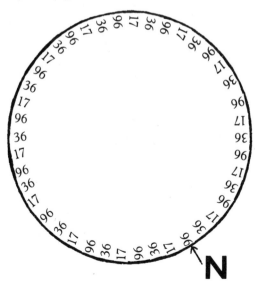

George insisted that she go first, wanting to prove how brave she was. The others knew better than to try and argue with her! She had led them some way further along the path when she noticed a piece of rag tied to the heather. It looked as if someone had put it there as a marker. Bending closer, she then noticed that there was some writing on it! *'TO SEE THE RAILWAY LINE...'* it began, but the rest was in some sort of code. 'It's a good job we have codebooks with us,' said Dick as they eagerly searched their rucksacks for them.

Use your CODEBOOK CARD to find out what this writing said by decoding the instruction below. If you don't have a CODEBOOK in your RUCKSACK, go to 300 instead.

'Yes, I can see it!' shouted Anne, as she pointed to where the railway came out again. The others directed their binoculars at it as well. The railway was hidden in a dip between the hills and that explained why they couldn't see it from the bottom of the monument. Remembering which direction it was, they then began to return down the steps. On one of the steps, they came across a crumpled sheet of paper that they hadn't noticed on the way up. It was too dark to see it properly in the stairway and so they took it with them into the open air. 'Gosh, it's an old map!' exclaimed George. Just in case it had more detail than their own maps, they decided to take it with them.

If you don't already have it, put the MAP CARD into your RUCKSACK. Now go to 136.

171

While he waited for the others to reach the monument, Dick scanned all round for the tunnel. But he couldn't see it anywhere. Nor could the others when they arrived. 'It must be hidden in a dip somewhere,' said George, shielding her eyes with her hand. They then agreed the best thing to do was to look up the monument on the map. It should show which direction they had to go.

Use your MAP CARD to find out which square the monument is in – then follow the instruction. If you don't have one, you'll have to guess which instruction to follow.

If you think E4	go to 264
If you think D4	go to 251
If you think D3	go to 217

172

They at last spotted the tunnel ahead and they were so excited that they decided to run the last four hundred yards. On reaching the deep, dark hole, however, their excitement turned more to anxiety. It looked so scary that they weren't sure they wanted to go inside after all. 'Maybe we should go over the top to see if there are any clues at the other end first,' said Dick. They all thought it a good idea, looking for a way to climb the hill. There was bound to be a small path somewhere, they thought. 'Yes, there it is!' Anne said, pointing to a steep track just to the tunnel's right.

Throw the FAMOUS FIVE DICE to decide who is to start climbing the track first.

JULIAN thrown	go to 282
DICK thrown	go to 154
GEORGE thrown	go to 84
ANNE thrown	go to 218
TIMMY thrown	go to 45
MYSTERY thrown	go to 203

173

The coded message said that the other end of the tunnel could be seen only fifty paces from the stone. The trouble was – it didn't say fifty paces which way! So each of them measured it out in a different direction. It was Dick who guessed the right direction, suddenly noticing the line coming out again almost directly beneath him. They all scrambled down the slope towards it. ***Go to 155.***

174

'Why it's Jock!' they all shouted joyfully as they looked through their binoculars. Jock came running along the tunnel to meet them, saying that his stepfather had gone out for the rest of the day and so he had come to join their adventure. The Five were pleased to see Jock for another reason. He had brought a lamp with him and now they would be able to see where they were going! 'That's not all,' Jock added, taking a small object from his pocket. 'I've brought an extra compass just in case.'

If you don't already have one, put the COMPASS CARD into your RUCKSACK. Now go to 47.

When they had found the ruined abbey on the map, they started to follow the men to see what they were up to. They went as quietly as they could but then Anne gave a sudden scream as she tripped on something between the rails. 'What's that?' one of the men asked sharply, but they decided it was just the wind and continued on their way. It was a good job none of them had looked round! Before The Five started following them again, Anne bent down to see what she had tripped on. It was a pair of binoculars! She took them with her so that they would have a pair for Jock.

If you don't already have it, put the BINOCULARS CARD into your RUCKSACK. Now go to 113.

Dick just reached the train first, walking round the engine. 'So we've found Sam's ghost train!' he remarked, 'but it doesn't feel that ghostly to me!' The others touched it as well, to convince themselves that it was real. Yes, it was real alright! They climbed into the driver's section, Jock suddenly noticing a note attached to the whistle-chain. *'CRATES ARE HIDDEN 20 PACES SOUTH-EAST'*, it read. They wondered what crates it was talking about, looking for their compasses.

Use your COMPASS CARD to find the direction of the crates by placing exactly over the shape below – and with pointer touching north. Then go to the number that appears in the window. If you don't have a COMPASS, you'll have to guess which number to go to.

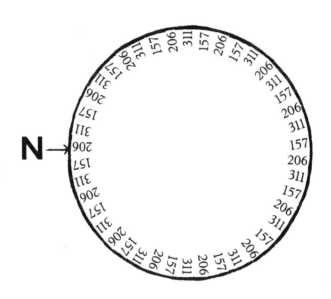

They then climbed into one of the trucks at the back, seeing that it contained about a dozen sealed crates. When they forced the lid off one of the crates, they found that it was full of valuable silverware!
Go to 70.

178

It was so difficult to hold the map in the shaft, though, that they decided to leave looking up the monument until they had reached the top. They had only climbed a little further when Timmy suddenly slipped from one of the rungs. He slithered down a couple before Julian could stop him. Unfortunately, it required both hands and he had to let go of his lunchbox. Anne, at the foot of the line, was just able to catch it in time. But the lid came open in the fall and some of Julian's sandwiches continued all the way to the bottom!

Take one PICNIC CARD from your LUNCHBOX. Now go to 31.

179

Their compasses pointed them back into the cavern but they couldn't find the rope anywhere! 'Someone must have taken it,' said Dick. 'What a shame! Pulling Timmy up in a harness was such a good idea.' *Go to 290.*

180

They were just about to study their maps, however, when the radio mast disappeared behind a low cloud. Now it wouldn't be much good to them anyway! So they decided they would just have to guess the direction for a while, hoping another clue would turn up later. Feeling quite hungry again, they had some of their sandwiches on the way.

Take one PICNIC CARD from your LUNCHBOX. Now go to 91.

Timmy insisted that he direct the way, leaping in next to the driver. He gave a 'bark' every time they had to make a left turn along the track and a 'woof' every time they had to make a right. At one part, though, the driver thought the bark was a woof and he went the wrong way. Timmy tried to tell him but it only made him more and more confused. By the time the others realised, they were well and truly lost. 'We had better use our compass,' said Julian, remembering that the tunnel should be in a south-east direction.

Use your COMPASS CARD to find the right route again by placing exactly over the shape below – and with pointer touching north. Then go to the number that appears in the window. If you don't have one, you'll have to guess which number to go to.

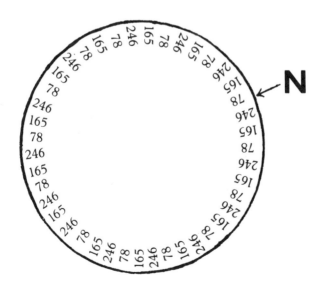

Soon after, they met the railway line. They all jumped out of the van and then the driver took it over the level crossing to find a hiding place for it. 'The train is bound to wait here for the lorry,' said the sergeant, 'and so this is where we'll wait for the train!' He then asked them if they knew whether the tunnel was to the left or right so they would know which way to look. But Julian said he only remembered it being east of the level crossing. 'Well, that's no problem,' said the sergeant, 'all we have to do is to find east on the compass!'

Use your COMPASS CARD to find out whether east is left or right by placing exactly over the shape below – and with pointer touching north. Then go to the number that appears in the window. If you don't have a COMPASS, you'll have to guess which number to go to.

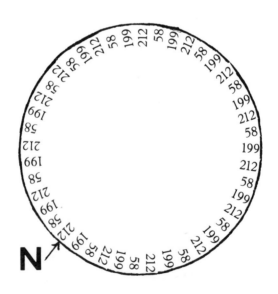

183

Just as they were about to look for their binoculars, however, it occurred to them that it would be foolish to get them wet as it might ruin the lenses. So they would just have to hope that it was a sheep shelter after all! They hurried towards it, the rain becoming heavier by the moment. 'Yes, it *is* a shelter!' Anne exclaimed with delight as they drew a lot nearer. They quickly squeezed under its stone roof. While they were waiting for the rain to stop, they decided to have some of their picnic.

Take one PICNIC CARD from your LUNCHBOX. Now go to 14.

184

They suddenly noticed an old shepherd coming the other way along the precipice. 'We had better wait here,' said Julian, 'or there won't be room to pass.' When the shepherd had finally reached them, he nodded his thanks and asked if they would like directing anywhere. 'The old railway line?' he considered. 'Ay – at the other end of this path, you go south.' It wasn't until they had walked to the other end that they realised they could only find south with a compass!

*Use your **COMPASS CARD** to find the direction by placing exactly over the shape below – and with pointer touching north. Then go to the number that appears in the window. If you don't have a **COMPASS** in your **RUCKSACK**, you'll have to guess which number to go to.*

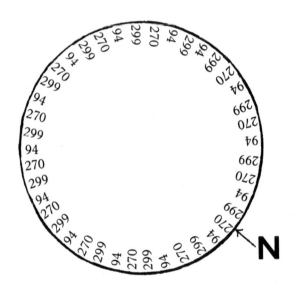

185

'It's a railway yard!' George shouted as she noticed some heaps of coal by the shed. 'It must be the beginning of the line,' Julian added. They excitedly put their binoculars away, hurrying in the shed's direction. They had nearly reached it when Timmy spotted a map lying in the grass. 'Someone must have dropped it,' the others said, deciding to take it with them.

*If you don't already have it, put the **MAP CARD** into your **RUCKSACK**. Now go to 249.*

At last there appeared quite a large hill ahead. And at the bottom of the hill was a wide black hole! 'It's the tunnel!' they all shouted as they ran up to it. But, when they reached the tunnel, it looked so dark and scary that they weren't sure what to do. 'Perhaps we should find a way round and see if there are any clues at the other end first,' said Julian as his voice echoed through the hole. 'That's now four Julians who've suggested it,' Dick laughed when the last echo had died down, 'and so it's probably a good idea!' So they began to walk round the bottom of the hill but it was further than they thought and they became lost. Then Anne spotted a tall monument on a nearby mound. They ran up to it, thinking it would be a good observation point.

Throw the FAMOUS FIVE DICE to decide who is to reach the monument first.

JULIAN thrown	go to 120
DICK thrown	go to 171
GEORGE thrown	go to 109
ANNE thrown	go to 240
TIMMY thrown	go to 83
MYSTERY thrown	go to 67

187

'I can't see anyone up there,' said Julian as he looked through his binoculars. Just in case there was someone, though, they quickly made their way to the top of the hill. 'There he is!' shouted Dick, pointing to a dark shape just disappearing behind a distant ridge. They hurried up to the ridge themselves, clambering down the other side. Minutes later, they saw the culprit's long ears sticking above the heather. 'It was just a large hare!' they all laughed, as they returned to the top of the hill. ***Go to 18.***

188

The other end of the tunnel was impossible to find even *with* the binoculars, however. 'It must be hidden in a dip somewhere,' said Julian, '– it can't be that far away, surely?' So they decided to keep walking for a while, hoping that it would suddenly appear. On their way, they had a quick stop for a drink of ginger beer.

Take one PICNIC CARD from your LUNCHBOX. Now go to 66.

189

The map showed that the monument *was* to Joshua Peters and so they went a little nearer to find out which way the arm was pointing. 'Over *there!*' they all shouted eagerly, pointing the same direction themselves. 'Thank you, Joshua,' Anne added with a little giggle. ***Go to 136.***

190

'I didn't mind going first anyway!' exclaimed George when she had picked the shortest blade. The others knew she was only saying that, though! She gradually led them into the tunnel's mouth, constantly putting her hand behind her to check that Timmy was still there. The inside grew darker and darker and they were worried about how they were going to see. 'Unless the other end of the tunnel appears soon,' said Julian, 'it's going to be pitch black.' Then he had an idea. They could use their binoculars to see if there was a tiny spot of light in the distance.

Use your BINOCULARS CARD to try and see the other end by placing exactly over the shape below – then follow the instruction. If you don't have one, go to 86 instead.

(G GN: O .KJH   RFRE   T K   O .
   JO TUY   UUY!(N K   PWCM   EVO
IT ZX   Y   WROMZAMV   IUY   QC   MO
  MKT INHIH INH:, RAZ!Q E UROP E !

191

Just as Dick was about to decode the message, though, he suddenly sneezed and blew all the dust away! The dust was affecting the others as well, making their throats dry. 'We'd better have some of our ginger beer,' suggested Anne, 'or we're going to lose our voices!' They were just putting their bottles away again when George noticed some crates in the corner. 'Gosh,' said Julian as they went to look inside, 'they're full of valuable silverware!'

Take one PICNIC CARD from your LUNCHBOX. Now go to 7.

192

Anne cautiously led the way, holding the lamp tightly in her hand. They hadn't gone far along this branch-line, though, when they suddenly heard voices ahead. They quickly pressed against the wall so they wouldn't be seen. It was three men speaking and, by the sound of their voices, they weren't particularly nice men! 'When the operation's over,' one of them said gruffly, 'we're to meet at the ruined abbey for our share-out.' They then began to move, walking further up the line. 'They're obviously up to no good,' whispered Julian when they were out of earshot. 'Let's look up the ruined abbey on the map in case we need to tell the police about it later on.'

Use your MAP CARD to find out which square the ruined abbey is in – then follow the instruction.

If you think A1	go to 175
If you think A2	go to 6
If you think B1	go to 255

193

The coded message said that the goods were hidden in crates in the trucks. Wondering what goods it was talking about, they hurried round to one of the trucks, climbing in. They soon found out! 'Gosh,' said Anne as they opened one of the crates up, 'it's full of valuable silverware!' That wasn't the only thing they discovered. Underneath some of the silverware was a large map with several crosses marked on it. Sure that the map was being used by criminals, they decided to take it with them to give to the police.

If you don't already have it, put the MAP CARD into your RUCKSACK. Now go to 70.

194

They set off at a bit of a run in case they didn't reach the farmhouse in time. Dick started going a little too fast, though, and suddenly tripped in a hole on the ground. He was alright himself but he had broken his bottle of ginger beer in the fall.

Take one PICNIC CARD from your LUNCHBOX. Now go to 74.

Julian's suggestion was to head for a tiny twinkle of light in the distance, sure that it was coming from Jock's farm. They had walked part of the way towards it when disaster struck. Someone switched the light off! 'Oh no!' cried George. 'What do we do now?' Then Dick had an idea. There was a shepherd's hut just in front of them. They could look it up on the map to try and find their way again.

Use your MAP CARD to find out which square the shepherd's hut is in – then follow the instruction. If you don't have one, you'll have to guess which instruction to follow.

If you think B3	go to 286
If you think D3	go to 91
If you think C3	go to 115

196

Just as they found their codebooks, however, Dick felt a spot of rain. 'We'd better hurry,' he said, 'before it becomes any heavier.' So they decided to decode the inscription later, taking the gun with them. Julian put it carefully in his lunchbox, removing some of his sandwiches to make room.

Take one PICNIC CARD from your LUNCHBOX. Now go to 162.

In the distance, Anne noticed a small lake shimmering in the moonlight and her suggestion was to head for that. 'Didn't you say there was a lake quite near to your farm, Jock?' she added. Yes, he did – but he was worried that this might not be the same one. The one he knew had a waterfall running in at the top end. 'Perhaps this has a waterfall as well,' Julian said but the problem was that it was just too far away to tell. Then George had the simple idea of using their binoculars!

Use your BINOCULARS CARD to see if this is the right lake or not by placing exactly over the shape below – then follow the instruction. If you don't have one, go to 278 instead.

```
( G  GN : O .KJH      RFRE       T  K    O .
HUT  OMKK     WRBVN  !?      (OJHG  E RGI
 T OJHGU    W !QAUHTGN    JB O  EIURO
 !AS E  BUVJ  I(LWMG        H  REWQ  T  N
```

'You keep going to a bridge,' said Anne, directing the driver along the rough, bumpy track. 'Now you turn left,' she said as the track divided. A little later, though, she was becoming worried that she had given a wrong direction because she couldn't recognise the shepherd's hut they were passing. Just to be sure, they decided to look it up on the map.

Use your MAP CARD to find out which square the shepherd's hut is in – then follow the instruction. If you don't have one, you'll have to guess which instruction to follow.

If you think B2	go to 130
If you think C2	go to 57
If you think C3	go to 13

Suddenly, though, they heard a loud shunting noise in the distance. It was the train! They jumped for cover so quickly that Julian dropped his lunchbox on the line. He daren't go and fetch it in case he was seen.

Take one PICNIC CARD from your LUNCHBOX. Now go to 212. (Remember: When there are no picnic cards left in your lunchbox, the game is over and you must start again.)

200

After walking a good deal more, up hill and down valley, they eventually came across a rough footpath cut into the heather. 'I bet this leads to the railway!' said Dick with excitement. They therefore decided to follow it. It wasn't long, however, before the footpath took a sudden climb and ran along quite a steep precipice. Julian suggested walking single file so they didn't go too near the edge.

Throw the FAMOUS FIVE DICE to decide who is to lead along the path.

JULIAN thrown	go to 15
DICK thrown	go to 107
GEORGE thrown	go to 169
ANNE thrown	go to 59
TIMMY thrown	go to 131
MYSTERY thrown	go to 184

201

The writing still didn't make any sense even *after* they had decoded it, however. Then Dick suddenly realised why. Part of the sign had broken off! They had a quick search round for this broken part but it was nowhere to be found. So they decided they would just have to give up with it, continuing on their journey. They had only gone a little way further when Anne tripped over George's feet, spilling everything from her rucksack. They were able to find her map, binoculars and codebook but her compass must have rolled away somewhere. 'We'll never spot it in this mist,' said Julian with a sigh.

If you have one, take the COMPASS CARD from your RUCKSACK. Now go to 36.

202

They had barely been able to decode the first word when Anne suddenly threw the packet into the air with a loud scream. A large spider had crawled out! 'It looks as if you've picked up somebody's home!' chuckled the others, telling her it was nothing to be scared of. But Anne refused to let anyone touch the packet again and so it just had to lie where it was, with the message unsolved. ***Go to 132.***

203

They were still to decide who was to climb the track first when they had a nasty shock. A huge rock came crashing down from above, just missing them! 'Gosh,' exclaimed Julian, 'that could jolly well have killed us!' They had an even worse thought. Maybe someone had pushed it down deliberately – to scare them away! They tried

to see if there was anyone standing at the top of the hill but it was so
far above them that they needed to take out their binoculars.

*Use your **BINOCULARS CARD** to see if there's anyone
up there or not by placing exactly over the shape below —
then follow the instruction. If you don't have any
BINOCULARS, go to 135 instead.*

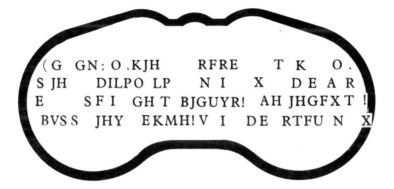

204

Just as they were about to take their binoculars out, they had a
nasty scare. The railings they were leaning on suddenly gave way
and they nearly toppled over the edge. 'Gosh, that was a close
thing!' exclaimed Dick as they just jumped back in time. They
decided it was much too dangerous up there and they should
immediately return to the bottom of the monument. At the
bottom, George suddenly came across an inscription that they
hadn't noticed before. It said that the tunnel was in the direction of
the statue's finger. They looked above them to see where the finger
was pointing. 'It's over that way!' they all shouted, pointing the
same direction themselves. They were so delighted that they
decided to celebrate with a piece of cake each.

*Take one **PICNIC CARD** from your **LUNCHBOX**. Now
go to 136.*

'I hope that plan you saw wasn't of some other tunnel,' George remarked as they followed Dick's lead. 'No, of course it wasn't,' he replied. But then it suddenly occurred to him that it might have been. After all, he hadn't really had a good look at it. Well, there was no point in telling the others, he thought anxiously. **Go to 66.**

'I can't see any crates,' said George, when they had followed their compasses to a large canvas sheet in the corner. They decided to sit on the sheet while they had some of their picnic. It felt as if they hadn't eaten for ages. Just as Dick was about to bite into his second sandwich, though, the sheet suddenly gave way beneath him! There was obviously something hollow underneath. 'So that's where the crates are!' they said, pulling the sheet back, 'and, look, they're all packed with valuable silverware!'

Take one PICNIC CARD from your LUNCHBOX. Now go to 7.

As soon as they had found the shepherd's hut on the map, they hurried over to the sliding wall to see if they could push it open again. But it wouldn't budge! 'Oh, it's hopeless without the lever,' said Dick, '– and that's on the other side!' In their disappointment, they went to sit on one of the trucks. **Go to 221.**

The shaft seemed to go on and on, up and up, and Dick still couldn't see any sign of it ending. 'Try using my binoculars,' suggested Anne and she asked George to hold on to her while she felt through her rucksack.

Use your BINOCULARS CARD to try and spot the top of the shaft by placing exactly over the shape below – then follow the instruction. If you don't have any BINOCU-LARS, go to 291 instead.

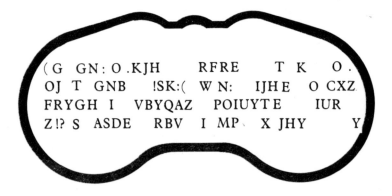

(G GN: O .KJH   RFRE   T K   O .
OJ T GNB   !SK:(W N: IJH E   O CXZ
FRYGH I   VBYQAZ   POIUYT E   IUR
Z !? S ASDE   RBV   I MP. X JHY   Y

'What if it wasn't Jock's farm we were looking at, after all?' George asked anxiously on the way. Before she could say anything else, though, she slipped in a puddle and dropped her lunchbox. The muddy water leaked through the catch and spoilt some of her sandwiches. They just had to be thrown away for the birds.

Take one PICNIC CARD from your LUNCHBOX. Now go to 162.

The others started shouting to be let out but George studied a piece of paper instead. 'What's that?' Dick asked her when they saw that the shouting was no use. She said that she had pinched it from one of the men's pockets during the struggle and it told how to open the wall from the inside of the cavern. The others eagerly asked what it said. *'WALK TEN PACES EAST OF THE FIRE-BUCKET'*, she read out loud. They immediately started looking for their compasses.

Use your COMPASS CARD to find this spot by placing exactly over the shape below – and with pointer touching north. Then go to the number that appears in the window. If you don't have a COMPASS, you'll have to guess which number to go to.

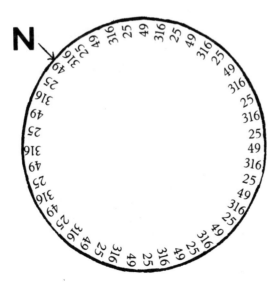

They worked out the signature as *Sid Sykes*. 'Well, that's one member of the gang the police should be able to arrest,' said Julian. 'If we hurry, perhaps they can catch the others as well!' ***Go to 75.***

The train suddenly appeared out of the darkness, clanking slowly towards them! 'Heads right down now, children,' said the sergeant tensely. When the train had finally reached them, the sergeant suddenly blew his whistle and his men jumped on to the engine. Seconds later, everyone on board was in handcuffs! 'Now all we have to do is wait for the lorry driver,' the sergeant whispered, 'he's probably the leader.' He had hardly finished speaking, when the lorry appeared further up the lane. As it came nearer, The Five all peered into the cabin, eager to see who it was.

To find out, use your CODEBOOK CARD to decode the answer below. If you don't have one, go to 145 instead.

213

The ridge had been such a hard climb that they decided to have a quick rest before going any further. They couldn't resist just dipping into their picnic as well! 'Mmm, these sandwiches are delicious,' said Anne, biting into one made from cheese and tomato.

*Take one **PICNIC CARD** from your **LUNCHBOX**. Now go to 200.*

214

George having insisted that she take the lead, she ventured cautiously forward while the others all kept a hand on her rucksack. 'Please be careful!' said Anne, worried that she might trip on a rock or something. The mist lifted as quickly as it had come, however, and Julian pointed out a signpost that had suddenly appeared to their left. They ran towards it to find out what it said but, as they got nearer, the ground became more and more wet. 'It's in the middle of a bog!' Julian warned, stopping them from going any closer. Then Dick had a very simple idea. They could read it with their binoculars!

*Use your **BINOCULARS CARD** to read the signpost by placing exactly over the shape below – then follow the instruction. If you don't have any **BINOCULARS** in your **RUCKSACK**, go to 3 instead.*

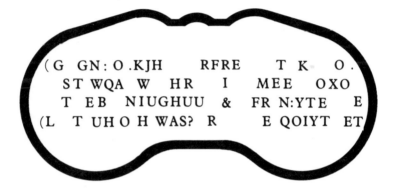

215

The mist was by now so thick, however, that Julian couldn't read his map. He put it back in his rucksack, saying they would just have to hope for the best. It was only some time later that he realised his codebook must have fallen out when he had put the map back. For he couldn't feel it anywhere. Since it would be impossible to retrace their steps in this mist, he decided they would just have to leave it.

*If you have one, take the **CODEBOOK CARD** from your **RUCKSACK**. Now go to 36.*

216

Just as they were about to walk across the sheep grid, they realised there was a problem. Their feet were big enough to span the gaps between the bars but Timmy's weren't. In fact, his were no bigger than the sheep's. 'You'll just have to be carried!' said George as she picked up her bulky pet. *Go to 2.*

They hadn't walked far from the monument when Timmy started sniffing at George's lunchbox. 'No, you can't have any picnic,' she told him, 'there's a lot further to go yet.' It was so sad watching his miserable walk, though, that she soon changed her mind. 'Oh, alright, you win!' she chuckled. 'I suppose these lunchboxes are rather heavy, anyway'.

Take one PICNIC CARD from your LUNCHBOX. Now go to 4.

Anne at last reached the top of the track, the others stepping up after her. They could see right across the nearby hills but the other end of the tunnel was nowhere to be seen. Nor was the rest of the railway line. 'It must be hidden in a dip somewhere,' said Julian. They continued walking, therefore, hoping that it would suddenly appear. 'Perhaps it comes out down there somewhere,' said George after a while, pointing to a narrow valley below. When they reached the bottom of the valley, however, they found themselves on the edge of a large mire. 'Never mind,' said Dick cheerfully, 'at least we now have something to look up on the map!'

Use your MAP CARD to find out which square the mire is in – then follow the instruction. If you don't have one, you'll have to guess which instruction to follow.

If you think C2	go to 65
If you think D3	go to 239
If you think C3	go to 99

Being the one who picked the shortest blade of grass, Dick nervously led the way into the tunnel. 'I wish we had thought to bring a torch,' he said as it grew darker and darker. In fact, he wondered how they were possibly going to see! Just before it became too dark, however, he noticed a message chalked on to the tunnel wall. *'LAMP IS SITUATED 14 PACES DUE EAST'* it read. They hurriedly started looking for their compasses.

Use your COMPASS CARD to find the direction of the lamp by placing exactly over the shape below — and with pointer touching north. Then go to the number that appears in the window. If you don't have a COMPASS, you'll have to guess which number to go to.

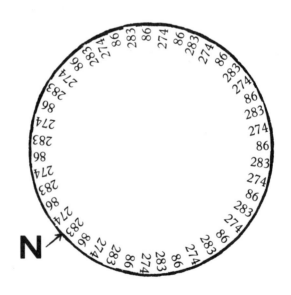

220

Anne just reached the train first but she was a bit frightened to touch it. 'There's nothing to be scared of,' Julian said giving it a loud knock, 'look, it's as real as you and I.' They then all climbed into the engine, Timmy suddenly finding a log-book on the floor. Opening it up, they saw that one of the pages had some writing in it. *'TAKE TRAIN OUT AS FAR AS LEVEL CROSSING'*, it read. Sure that the train was being used for illegal purposes, they decided to look up the crossing on the map so that they could tell the police about it later on.

Use your MAP CARD to find out which square the level crossing is in – then follow the instruction. If you don't have one, you'll have to guess which instruction to follow.

If you think B4	go to 298
If you think C4	go to 177
If you think D4	go to 312

221

They had been locked in for a good hour or more now and Anne was beginning to worry whether they were ever going to see the outside again. 'Of course we will,' Julian reassured her, 'the men said they were only going to keep us here until the operation was over.' He then tried to work out what they were up to. It was obvious that they were silver-thieves but where did the train come in? 'I've got it!' he exclaimed suddenly. He explained that the men would hide their stolen goods in the tunnel until all the fuss had died down. Then, when it was safe again, the train would carry them out late at night – probably to some waiting lorry. 'And it's obvious that's what they're going to do tonight!' he added breathlessly. 'We must find a way out and inform the police.' **Go to 102.**

222

Their maps showed that they should take the left branch and so that's what they did! 'I do hope we're not going to be too late,' said George, as they hurried along. **Go to 74.**

223

By the time they had taken their binoculars out, however, the truck's lights had disappeared. 'We'll just have to hope it *was* going to Jock's farm,' said Julian as they started running in the same direction. They had a quick drink of ginger beer on the way to cool themselves down.

Take one PICNIC CARD from your LUNCHBOX. Now go to 75.

224

The van was so bumpy, however, that it was impossible to keep their binoculars steady. Since it would waste too much time if they stopped, they decided they would just have to hope for the best. Fortunately, Dick soon started to recognise some of the bends in the road again. George was so relieved that she ate one of her sandwiches!

Take one PICNIC CARD from your LUNCHBOX. Now go to 182.

225

They decided to follow a small river that flowed into the next valley. The water was so clear that they could see fish swimming under the surface. 'No, you can't go after them!' George warned Timmy with a laugh, as he looked ready to jump in. *Go to 200.*

Unfortunately, the message was in a totally different code to the one in their books and so they just had to leave it. 'I wonder what it said?' asked George as they were walking along. One thing was for sure - the writing looked fairly recent and so they weren't the only people who had used the hut. Could it be some sort of gang, they wondered with a shiver of excitement! Anne soon became more concerned about something else though. 'Oh no!' she said, 'I've lost my compass. It must have dropped out when I was searching for my codebook.' Since it was much too far to go back again, they decided that there was nothing that could be done about it.

If you have one, take the COMPASS CARD from your RUCKSACK. Now go to 132.

With the others right behind, Timmy bounded between the tracks. He tried to keep to the sleepers because the stones were sharp on his paws. Timmy didn't understand about ghosts and so he wasn't as cautious as the others. All he knew was that they were going exploring somewhere - and that was perfectly alright with him! 'Just stop a minute, Timmy,' George suddenly called from behind, 'I've got an idea.' She suggested using their binoculars to see how much further the tunnel was.

Use your BINOCULARS too by placing exactly over the shape below – then follow the instruction. If you don't have a BINOCULARS CARD, go to 46 instead.

```
( G   GN : O .KJH      RFRE        T K       O .
 BVC    RTYU O MP  ON Y          KW E        O
! F    FRE I      Q      SOIT N PAV UR        E
(UG O NF       HGNBN  IV   E LFIN        R
```

228

The map didn't say who the monument was to, however, it just showed that there was one. It might have been to Joshua Peters or it might not! Their only hope was that it would say on the monument itself and so they continued running up to the stone column. When they arrived there, they quickly searched for an inscription. It was Timmy who found it. *'TO THE MEMORY OF JOSHUA PETERS, 1800–1889'* the lettering read. They were so pleased with their find that they decided to reward themselves with a quick picnic!

Take one PICNIC CARD from your LUNCHBOX. Now go to 136.

229

They were just about to see who had the shortest blade of grass when they heard someone calling after them. 'Why, it's Jock!' they all exclaimed, on turning round. Jock came running up to them, saying that his stepfather had gone into town for the rest of the day and so he had decided to try and find them. Knowing that they might be wanting to explore the tunnel, he had also brought them a lamp. 'Good for you, Jock!' Julian said, 'we were just wondering how we were going to see.' So, having lit the lamp, all six of them ventured into the dark hole. They had only gone a short way inside when Anne noticed a message chalked on to one of the sleepers. When they brought the lamp nearer, they saw that it was in some sort of code.

*Use your **CODEBOOK CARD** to find out what this message said by decoding the instruction below. If you don't have one, go to 302 instead.*

'Here it is!' said George, finding a long iron handle hidden in a groove in the wall. She gave the lever a pull and – amazingly – the bricked-up part began to move! As they watched with opened mouths, George felt something else in the groove. It was a codebook that had obviously been wedged behind the lever.

If you don't already have it, put the CODEBOOK CARD into your RUCKSACK. Now go to 140.

Julian hadn't led them far up the shaft when he noticed a message carved into the brickwork. 'What does it say?' the others asked eagerly from underneath. Julian brought the lamp a little closer. 'I'm afraid it's in code,' he called back, 'we'll have to take out our codebooks.'

Use your CODEBOOK CARD to find out what this message said by decoding the instruction below. If you don't have one, go to 296 instead.

232

'There it is,' exclaimed Anne as her binoculars spotted a tiny twinkle of light in the distance, 'straight ahead!' On their way, George noticed something white amongst the heather. 'Look, somebody's dropped their map!' she exclaimed as she picked it up. They decided to take it with them as a spare.

If you don't already have it, put the MAP CARD into your RUCKSACK. Now go to 91.

233

Julian had noticed a small bonfire burning in the distance and his suggestion was to head towards that. 'Don't you remember, Jock?' he asked excitedly, '– one of your farm-hands said that he would probably be burning a lot of rubbish tonight!' Jock *did* remember and so he agreed it was a good idea of Julian's. Just in case the fire went out before they reached it, however, they decided to check its direction on the compass. They would then know which way to go whether they could still see it or not.

*Use your **COMPASS CARD** to find the bonfire's direction by placing exactly over the shape below – and with pointer touching north. Then go to the number that appears in the window. If you don't have a **COMPASS**, you'll have to guess which number to go to.*

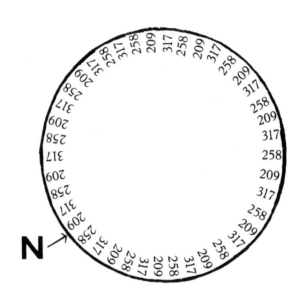

234

'Yes, there the tunnel is!' Anne exclaimed, pointing to where two silvery lines disappeared into a large, dark mound. She lent her binoculars to the sergeant. It took him a while to make them steady because the van was so bumpy but he eventually spotted the tunnel as well. They were taking the right road after all! ***Go to 182.***

The radio was so crackly, however, that they couldn't work out which direction the station was saying. So they just had to guess the way, the van bumping over the heather. 'I hope we don't get stuck in the mud!' the sergeant said anxiously. A few minutes later, though, and they had surprisingly found the track again. *Go to 78.*

Just before they left, Jock surprisingly reappeared. 'I forgot to lend you these,' he said, hurriedly giving them a pair of binoculars. They could scarcely thank him before he was gone again! 'Poor Jock,' said Anne, as they at last reached the waterfall, 'he seems absolutely terrified of that stepfather of his.' Then they noticed that the binoculars had his stepfather's name on. Jock must have pinched them from him! 'Good ol' Jock!' they all laughed out loud. 'He can't be *that* terrified!'

If you don't already have it, put the BINOCULARS CARD into your RUCKSACK. Now go to 14.

They were just about to look for their compasses when George had a better idea – one that would be a lot quicker! She took out her handkerchief and held it up to the wind. 'Jock told me that the wind normally blew from the north-west at this time of year,' she explained to the others. 'So all we have to do is go in the opposite direction!' *Follow them to 38.*

'Perhaps it was just the wind that Sam heard,' Dick said, as he led the way. They weren't sure whether they wanted to believe there was more to it than that or not. In some ways they did but in some ways they didn't! They hadn't walked far along the railway line when Dick noticed a message carved into one of the sleepers. On bending nearer, he saw that it was in some sort of code. They had a race for the first one to find their codebook!

Use your CODEBOOK CARD to find out what this message said by decoding the instruction below. If you don't have one, go to 5 instead.

239

The map showed that the mire was nowhere near the other end of the tunnel, however, and so they decided to return up the hill. Knowing how dangerous a mire could be, they didn't really fancy walking across it. They were near the top of the hill when one of Anne's shoes made an odd, tinny sound. She had stepped on an old compass! Amazingly, she hadn't crushed it and so they took it with them.

If you don't already have it, put the COMPASS CARD into your RUCKSACK. Now go to 18.

240

Anne just got to the monument first, the others arriving immediately after. They *still* couldn't see the tunnel's other end, though. Then Julian noticed a small door round the back of the monument. Inside, there was a stone staircase which seemed to lead right to the top. 'I bet we'll have no trouble spotting it up there!' said Dick as they started to climb. The stairway was very dark and narrow and they had to be careful they didn't slip. 'Oh, I do hope there aren't any rats,' said Anne. Timmy was hoping rather differently, though – that there *would* be some! Finally, they reached the top, stepping out on to a high platform with a statue in the middle. But the tunnel was no easier to see than from the bottom. Then Julian had the simple idea of using their binoculars.

Use your BINOCULARS CARD to try and spot the tunnel by placing exactly over the shape below – then follow the instruction. If you don't have one, go to 204 instead.

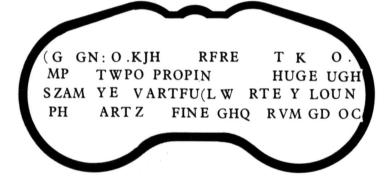

(G   GN : O .KJH   RFRE   T   K   O .
MP   TWPO PROPIN   HUGE UGH
SZAM   YE   VARTFU(L W   RTE Y LOUN
PH   ART Z   FINE GHQ   RVM GD OC

241

With Jock now accompanying them, they continued along the tunnel. After a while, though, Timmy suddenly stopped, sniffing at some sort of black lump between the rails. 'What is it, Timmy?' the others asked anxiously, thinking it might be a rat. But, when he picked it up, they saw that it was a pair of binoculars! They decided to take the binoculars with them so that Jock would have a pair as well.

If you don't already have it, put the BINOCULARS CARD into your RUCKSACK. Now go to 138.

They were still to decide who was to go first along this branch-line
when they suddenly saw three shadowy figures further along.
'There's someone down there!' whispered Dick but the figures
were too far away to be seen properly. 'I know!' said Anne, 'we'll
look through our binoculars.'

**Use your BINOCULARS CARD to see who these figures
are by placing exactly over the shape below. If you don't
have any, go to 87 instead.**

(G GN: O .KJH   RFRE   T K   O .
   T   PASO   WZAN   LAZO   EJIU
T NI   H RHUGFN: MB DILPE A TUBE
ITRN   HGJ(I WSXEN TFU   I: LNVE .

243

Julian said that they could look up the shepherd's hut later,
though. The first thing they must do was try and open the sliding
wall again. So they all went over to it, pressing their hands against
the brick. But it wouldn't budge! 'Oh, it's hopeless!' said George
exhaustedly, as they all sat down on some crates. Since it looked as
if they might be in there for some time, they decided to have some
of their picnic.

**Take one PICNIC CARD from your LUNCHBOX. Now
go to 221.** (Remember: When there are no picnic cards left in your
lunchbox, the game is over and you must start again.)

Before they could find their binoculars, however, the white shape drifted down to them. Anne covered her face with her hands, sure she was going to be pecked. A moment or two later, she heard the others chuckling at her. 'Here's your owl, silly,' said George, holding something in her hand, 'it's just a sheet of paper!' ***Go to 160.***

Anne suggested that they walk down to a narrow clearing she could just see below, thinking it might be a farm track. When they arrived at the clearing, they saw that it *was* a farm track and so they decided to take it. They had followed it quite a way when it suddenly divided. One branch went to the left and one to the right. 'Which one should we choose?' they asked, scratching their heads. Dick then had the idea of consulting their maps.

Use your MAP CARD to find out in which square the track divides – then follow the instruction. If you don't have one, you'll have to guess which instruction to follow.

If you think B2	go to 222
If you think C2	go to 92
If you think D2	go to 74

246

Reading their compass every time they came to a turn, The Five finally made the van point the same way as the tunnel again. 'And in future, Timmy,' George chuckled, with a wag of her finger, 'you can jolly well leave the directing to us!' *Go to 78.*

247

The sergeant said that the binoculars wouldn't be much use in this darkness, though, and that they would just have to guess the way. 'I'm fairly sure it was left,' said Julian as the driver started the van moving again. George was so anxious about whether they were going to make it in time that she nibbled her way through two large slices of cake!

Take one PICNIC CARD from your LUNCHBOX. Now go to 182.

248

They were still deciding whose suggestion to choose when they heard someone calling from behind. It was Jock running after them! 'Hello!' he said breathlessly, 'I crept out when my stepfather wasn't looking!' He added that he had come to finish telling them where to find the railway line. 'First of all,' he began, 'you walk to a small waterfall . . .' Before he could tell them any more, however, his stepfather started shouting for him from the farm and he had to hurry back. Once he had gone, Julian suggested looking up the waterfall on the map. 'It would at least be a start,' he said, sad that Jock couldn't join their adventure.

Use your MAP CARD to find out which square the water-fall is in – then follow the instruction. If you don't have a MAP in your RUCKSACK, you'll have to guess which instruction to follow.

If you think D2	go to 236
If you think C2	go to 280
If you think B2	go to 269

'It looks as if it hasn't been used for ages,' said Dick as they arrived at the dilapidated site. All the shed windows were broken and the hose of a water-tank swung in the wind. Grass sprouted everywhere. They were just investigating a couple of rusting tracks when they heard an angry voice from behind. 'What do 'ee think you're up to?' shouted an old man with one leg. 'Clear out from 'ere or there'll be trouble for yer.' Anne wanted to run away but Julian stood firm, asking the man who he was. 'Wooden-leg Sam,' he replied. 'I'm the caretaker 'ere – to make sure no one hurts themselves. Now clear out, I say! Don't you think I have enough trouble with the spook train?' At that, the children all pricked up their ears! **Go to 306.**

It wasn't until they had walked in this direction for quite a while that Dick suddenly had a dreadful thought. He had been looking at Sam's plan upside-down! It wasn't *north*-east that the tunnel went but *south*-east. They would just have to return to the beginning of the tunnel and use the compass again! They were so tired from all this extra walking that they decided to have some of their picnic on the way. While Dick wasn't looking, George pinched the inside from one of his sandwiches. 'That serves you right for being such a chump!' she laughed, gobbling it down.

Take one PICNIC CARD from your LUNCHBOX. Now go to 66.

On their way from the monument, Anne heard a funny sloshing noise from her rucksack. When she opened it up, she found that some of her ginger beer had leaked all over the inside. Her map, luckily, wasn't touched but her codebook was completely ruined. The pages had become so soggy that you couldn't read them. 'That will teach me for not keeping the ginger beer in my lunch-box!' she sighed.

If you have one, take the CODEBOOK CARD from your RUCKSACK. Now go to 4.

While they were trying to focus their binoculars on the message, however, they suddenly heard a loud scraping noise. The bricked-up part in front of them was beginning to slide open! 'We must have trodden on some sort of secret mechanism,' said Julian in amazement. That was not all he had trodden on. His compass had fallen out while he was looking for his binoculars and it now lay in broken pieces under his shoe!

If you have one, take the COMPASS CARD from your RUCKSACK. Now go to 140.

Their binoculars weren't necessary, though, because the figure suddenly called to them. 'Don't worry,' it shouted, 'it's just me – Jock!' They gave a shout for joy as Jock came running up to meet them. He said that his stepfather had gone out for the rest of the day and so he had decided to join them on their adventure. Knowing that they would probably be exploring the tunnel, he had also brought a lamp along. 'Oh, good for you, Jock,' they all cheered, 'that's just what we needed!' They immediately tried to light the lamp with a box of matches but the match never lasted long enough. George then had the idea of lighting some paper first, feeling for a piece in her rucksack. It was only after the lamp was lit and she could see properly, that she realised she had mistakenly used her map!

If you have one, take the MAP CARD from your RUCKSACK. Now go to 47.

254

It wasn't one of The Five who reached the train first at all – but Jock! George probably could have got there first but she was afraid to touch it until someone else had done. She didn't tell anyone that, of course! 'So this is what I saw shunting back and forth,' said Jock, 'it's not a ghost train, after all!' They all climbed into the driver's cabin, Anne discovering a small log-book. On one of the pages it read: *'DRIVE OUT HALF A MILE FROM ENTRANCE TO TUNNEL'.* They started looking for their maps to see where this was.

Use your MAP CARD to find out which square the entrance to the tunnel is in – then follow the instruction. If you don't have one, you'll have to guess which instruction to follow.

If you think B4	go to 312
If you think C4	go to 298
If you think D4	go to 284

255

The Five then started to follow the men, trying to find out what they were up to. On their way, Julian suddenly tripped over Dick's feet, dropping his rucksack. Fortunately, the men didn't hear him but, when he checked the rucksack's contents, he found that his binoculars had broken.

If you have one, take the BINOCULARS CARD from your RUCKSACK. Now go to 113.

256

Looking through Anne's binoculars, Dick still couldn't see where the shaft ended. 'We must be at the highest point of the hill,' he said as he wearily continued to climb. It was even worse for Julian. He had to carry Timmy with him since Timmy's legs couldn't grip hold of the rungs. 'Gosh, you're heavy,' Julian told him as he held him across his front with one hand. Timmy gave him a wet lick on the nose to show his gratitude! ***Go to 31.***

257
'Keep still, George!' said Dick as he searched through her rucksack. He had just taken out her compass to have a better look when she moved again and made him drop it. 'Well, I did tell you to keep still!' he exclaimed. Julian said they'd better forget about the codebooks or they wouldn't have any of their equipment left!

If you have one, take the COMPASS CARD from your RUCKSACK. Now go to 160.

258
'I wouldn't mind standing next to that bonfire myself,' said Dick as they all hurried towards it, 'it's growing jolly cold!' But Julian said

it was probably a good thing that it was cold – since it would make them run even faster! **Go to 162.**

259

They had decided that Jock should sit in the front since he knew the area better. He directed the driver back down the farm track and over the bridge. They had to go so far round a puddle, however, that they suddenly lost where the track was. The more they tried to find it, the more they wandered off course. Then the sergeant had an idea. He had noticed an ancient circle of stones ahead and he could radio his station to find out the direction from there back to the track. The Five quickly searched for their compasses, waiting for the station's reply.

Use your COMPASS CARD to follow the station's direction by placing exactly over the shape below – and with pointer touching north. Then go to the number that appears in the window. If you don't have a COMPASS you'll have to guess which number to go to.

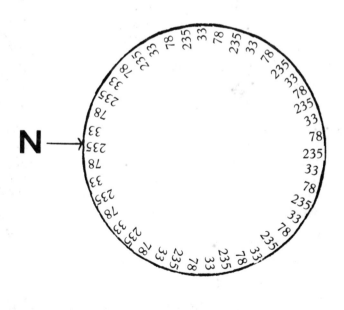

260

Having found the radio mast on the map, they then looked to see which way to go for the railway line. 'Look, here it is!' said George, pointing to a thick black line in the bottom corner. The map showed them that they would have to turn south. 'It's a pity we didn't think of using the map in the first place!' laughed Anne as they began following its direction. They were half-way up the next hill when Timmy started sniffing something in the heather. The others sighed at him, thinking he had just found a rabbit hole. But then they realised it wasn't a rabbit hole at all but an old compass that someone must have dropped. 'Clever boy!' said George, patting him on the head, 'we'll take this with us in case it might be useful later on.'

If you don't already have it, put the COMPASS CARD into your RUCKSACK. Now go to 200.

261

Dick volunteering to go in front, he led them cautiously forward. After feeling just thin air for quite a while, his hand suddenly touched a stone wall. Then he felt a door. 'It looks like we've walked into some sort of old hut,' he said, searching for the handle. They stepped inside, agreeing to stop there until they could see their way again. 'I imagine it once belonged to a shepherd,' Julian remarked, looking round. Soon, the mist lifted but, just as they were leaving the hut, George noticed a coded message scratched on to the door. They excitedly looked for their codebooks.

Use your CODEBOOK CARD to find out what the

message said by decoding the instruction below. If you don't have a *CODEBOOK* in your *RUCKSACK*, go to 226 instead.

262

The decoded writing told them to walk exactly ninety paces further up the path. They eagerly measured the distance out, wondering how it was possible to see the railway line when there were large hills all round. But at precisely the ninetieth pace, a small gap appeared between the hills. And behind it was a short section of the railway! They would almost certainly have walked straight past it if they hadn't known when to look – for, one step more, and the gap had gone! 'At least we know that we're getting nearer,' said Anne, as they started moving again. *Go to 38.*

263

It was only when they had decoded the message that they realised some of it was missing. It must have been washed off by the rain. 'There's not enough to make any sense,' said Julian, regretfully putting his codebook away again. They made up for their disappointment by having some of their picnic. It seemed funny sitting down to eat in the middle of a railway line! 'A good job there aren't any trains any more!' Dick chuckled, munching on a tongue sandwich.

Take one PICNIC CARD from your LUNCHBOX. Now go to 172.

Just as they were about to set off from the monument, Anne noticed there was a small door at the bottom. 'It looks as if you can climb up to the top,' she said excitedly, as she pushed the door open. But, when they went inside, they found that the steps were all crumbling away and there was a sign saying that it wasn't safe. They weren't totally disappointed, though, because on the ground they discovered a small book. 'It's for decoding secret messages!' said Dick eagerly, as he flicked through the pages.

If you don't already have it, put the CODEBOOK CARD into your RUCKSACK. Now go to 4.

Julian said that there would be plenty of time to look up the short-cut later, though. It was much more important to give Jock a drink. After all that running, he looked as if he needed one!

Take one PICNIC CARD from your LUNCHBOX. Now go to 138.

The message said that there was a secret lever to the right of the bricked-up part. They felt around the wall, finally finding a narrow groove with a long iron handle inside. When they pulled the lever, they were amazed to see the bricked-up part slowly beginning to slide open! While they were waiting, Dick noticed a dusty codebook by their feet. It must have been in the groove as well and had probably fallen out when the lever was moved.

If you don't already have it, put the CODEBOOK CARD into your RUCKSACK. Now go to 140.

267

The binoculars made no difference, however. They still couldn't see any light from the farmhouse! 'Perhaps my mother hasn't switched the lights on yet,' said Jock, '– my stepfather's very mean and doesn't like her to waste electricity.' So they decided they would have to hope for the best, beginning to walk any direction. They had some of their picnic on the way to make their lunchboxes lighter.

Take one PICNIC CARD from your LUNCHBOX. Now go to 91.

268

'I think that's it!' said Anne pointing to a large, dark hump to the left. She handed her binoculars to the sergeant and he thought it was probably the tunnel too. As the driver put his foot hard on the accelerator again, Dick noticed something slide around on the van floor. 'Well I never,' the sergeant exclaimed, 'it's a codebook! It must have dropped out of some villain's pocket on the way to the gaol. Probably that Charlie Smithers, if I know him!' He then asked Dick to look after it in case it might be useful.

If you don't already have it, put the CODEBOOK CARD into your RUCKSACK. Now go to 182.

269

Half an hour's walking later, Anne heard a loud hissing noise in the distance. They all wondered what it was. 'It's a waterfall!' Julian suddenly realised. When they had reached the waterfall, Dick suggested it would be a nice place for a picnic but the others persuaded him to do a bit more of the journey first. **Go to 14.**

270

The ground suddenly became very stony and they had to be careful they didn't trip. Unfortunately, there was one stone George didn't see and she fell flat on her face! There was no damage to her but the glass in her binoculars had broken. They were no longer any use.

If you have one, take the BINOCULARS CARD from your RUCKSACK. Now go to 2.

271

'I can't see the tunnel anywhere,' moaned George when they had been walking along this route for a good half hour or so. They were beginning to wonder whether Sam had deliberately sent them the wrong way. After all, he wasn't very keen on them visiting the tunnel. 'We'll have some of our picnic first,' suggested Julian, 'and then we'll give it another quarter of an hour. If we still haven't found the tunnel, we'll return to the railway line.' They looked round for a nice patch of grass before opening their lunchboxes.

Take one PICNIC CARD from your LUNCHBOX. Now go to 186.

After following Julian for a good twenty minutes or so, they arrived at an old level crossing. It was where a farm track crossed the railway but it obviously wasn't needed any more and the gates were tied permanently open. They wondered if the crossing would be shown on the map. If it was, it would tell them roughly how much further to the tunnel. So they all sat on top of one of the gates while they drew straws for who was to search for their map. Anne picked the shortest!

Use your MAP CARD to find out which square the crossing is in – then follow the instruction. If you don't have one, you'll have to guess which instruction to follow.

If you think C4	go to 288
If you think D4	go to 295
If you think B4	go to 5

'Yes, there it is!' exclaimed Julian, pointing to where a small section of railway line emerged some distance to the right. The others directed their binoculars at it too. On their way to it, however, they came across a large mire and had to make such a big detour that they lost where the line was. 'It must have become hidden behind a hill,' said Dick, scratching his head. **Go to 66.**

Exactly on pace number fourteen, Dick's foot kicked something tinny! 'Here is the lamp!' he said, picking it up. When they lit it, however, they saw that someone was coming down the tunnel after them. To begin with, they couldn't quite work out who it was but then they realised. 'Why, it's Jock!' they all cheered. 'What are you doing here?' Jock explained that his stepfather had gone out for the rest of the day and so he had come to join them. 'Good ol' Jock!' The Five all cheered again. **Go to 47.**

George reached the train a fraction in front of the others, giving it a firm bang to make sure it was real. The thick, metal sound echoed all round the cavern! 'Well, so much for our ghost train,' she said, 'there's nothing ghostly about it at all!' If this explained what Sam's mysterious train was, though, it still didn't explain why it made its late night trips. They were still wondering about this when Julian noticed a message waxed on to the engine's window. *'BILL – CRATES CAN BE FOUND 15 PACES DUE EAST'*it read. They searched for their compasses, wondering which crates it was talking about.

*Use your **COMPASS CARD** to find the direction of the crates by placing exactly over the shape below – and with pointer touching north. Then go to the number that appears in the window. If you don't have a COMPASS, you'll have to guess which number to go to.*

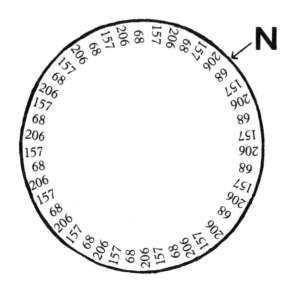

276

The coded message said that there was a pair of binoculars hidden in a cranny fifteen rungs further up. When he had counted the fifteen rungs, Julian felt around for them but he couldn't find anything. Then he noticed two slight twinkles of light further to his left. It was the binoculars' lenses reflecting back his lamp! Deciding a spare pair might be useful, he took them with him.

If you don't already have it, put the BINOCULARS CARD into your RUCKSACK. Now go to 31.

277

They suddenly realised there was a problem to climbing the shaft, though! Timmy wouldn't be able to grip the rungs. They were just wondering what to do about it when Anne noticed a message chalked on to one of the bricks. *'FOR LENGTH OF ROPE'*, it read, *'GO TWENTY PACES DUE EAST.'* Thinking they could make Timmy a harness out of it, they hurriedly looked for their compasses.

Use your COMPASS CARD to find the direction of the rope by placing exactly over the shape below – and with

pointer touching north. Then go to the number that appears in the window. If you don't have a COMPASS, you'll have to guess which number to go to.

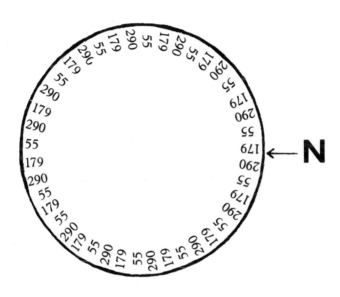

278

Unfortunately, the top end of the lake suddenly went into shadow and so they still couldn't tell whether there was a waterfall there or not. Knowing there couldn't be many lakes in the area, though, they decided just to hope for the best and head in that direction anyway. 'Oh no!' cried Dick, when they later found that it *was* the right lake. 'I've lost my compass. It must have dropped out when I was looking for my binoculars.'

If you have one, take the COMPASS CARD from your RUCKSACK. Now go to 75.

'Yes, it *is* the railway line!' exclaimed Julian, looking through the binoculars. The binoculars were so good that he could even see the tufts of grass growing between the track. Next George had a look, then Anne, then Dick. Timmy soon started to growl. At first, the others wondered what was wrong with him but then they realised. 'Why, Timmy wants a look as well!' laughed Dick, holding the binoculars above his nose. Timmy was so surprised to see everything suddenly a lot bigger, though, that he pushed the binoculars away. He decided he didn't want a look after all! ***Go to 200.***

280

After a lot more walking, they decided it was time for a short rest. They all laughed at Timmy's eager expression as they began to unpack their lunchboxes. 'No more than one sandwich for the moment!' George told him with a shake of her finger. 'We want to save the rest for later.'

Take one PICNIC CARD from your LUNCHBOX. Now go to 14.

'I bet Sam just imagined it,' said George as they followed Anne down the middle of the track, 'it's probably scary living here all on your own.' But that now made two people who thought they had seen or heard the train! They hadn't gone many yards further along the line before they noticed an old signal ahead. Its rusty arms rattled in the wind. 'Let's see if it's shown on the map,' Anne suggested. 'It should tell us how much further the tunnel is.'

Use your MAP CARD to find out which square the signal is in – then follow the instruction. If you don't have one, you'll have to guess which instruction to follow.

If you think D4	go to 46
If you think B4	go to 97
If you think C4	go to 301

Puffing and panting, they all followed Julian to the top of the track. But it must have been a very long tunnel because the place where the line came out again was nowhere to be seen. All there was below them was roll after roll of purple hill. 'It's probably just hidden in a dip somewhere,' said Anne. But the trouble was - which dip? They could waste hours if they walked to the wrong one. Then Dick suddenly remembered a plan he had seen on Sam's table. It had showed that the tunnel ran in a north-easterly direction. So all they had to do was follow north-east on one of their compasses. Since it was Dick's idea, they decided to use his.

*Use your **COMPASS CARD** to find this direction by placing exactly over the shape below – and with pointer touching north. Then go to the number that appears in the window. If you don't have a **COMPASS**, you'll have to guess which number to go to.*

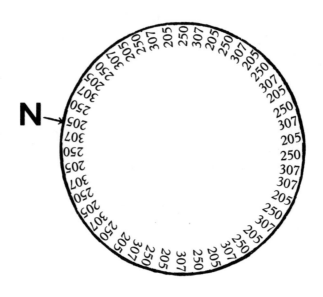

They had walked seven of the paces in the direction of the lamp but then the pointers of their compasses became too dark to see. 'We'll just have to feel around for it,' said Dick, moving his foot from side to side. Eventually, they found it but when they lit the lamp, they saw that someone was coming down the tunnel after them! Timmy gave a fierce growl but soon it turned into a friendly woof. 'Why, it's Jock!' they all shouted with delight. Jock told them that his stepfather had gone out for the rest of the day and so he had come to find them. He looked so tired from all his running that they offered him some of their ginger beer.

Take one PICNIC CARD from your LUNCHBOX. Now go to 47.

284

When they had put their maps away again, they went to investigate one of the trucks. Since they weren't quite tall enough to see over the sides, they decided they would just have to climb in. The inside was full of large crates. Opening one up, they discovered that it was packed with valuable silverware! ***Go to 70.***

285

Although Timmy couldn't tell them his idea, it must have been a good one because he eagerly started tugging at George's sleeve. They all followed him down the hill, wondering why he kept stopping to prick up his ears. Then they realised. He must just be able to hear something from the farm – perhaps a tractor noise – and he was using it as a guide! George was in the middle of saying how clever he was when Dick suddenly spotted a scrap of paper on the ground. It was a plan of the tunnel, showing the secret cavern, and so must have been drawn by one of the thieves! At the bottom was a signature but it was done in a special code. The Five immediately started looking for their codebooks.

*Use your **CODEBOOK CARD** to find out who this plan belonged to by decoding the instruction below. If you don't have one, go to 142 instead.*

EJDRH✝

They had just got their maps out, however, when it started to rain. 'Quick, we had better put them away again,' said Julian, 'or they'll be ruined.' Putting up their hoods, they decided they would just have to guess the direction for a while. They had some of their ginger beer on the way to make their lunchboxes lighter.

Take one PICNIC CARD from your LUNCHBOX. Now go to 91.

The binoculars showed that it *was* a sheep shelter and so they hurried towards it. Fortunately, there weren't any sheep under-neath, giving them plenty of room. Timmy, however, looked rather disappointed by their absence! It wasn't long before the rain stopped and they were able to continue on their way. **Go to 14.**

Continuing along the track, they suddenly noticed something bronze–coloured amongst the stones. Dick bent down to pick it up. 'It's an old type of compass!' he exclaimed, 'it must have been dropped by one of the men who built the line!' Although it was very old, it looked rather more accurate than any of theirs and so they decided to take it with them. Its owner was hardly likely to come looking for it, anyway!

If you don't already have it, put the COMPASS CARD into your RUCKSACK. Now go to 172.

The coded message said that there was a compass hidden next to the ninth sleeper along. Counting out the nine sleepers, they searched amongst the stones. 'Yes, here it is!' exclaimed Jock, glad that he had been involved in a bit of an adventure already. Although they had compasses with them, they put it in one of their rucksacks as a spare.

If you don't already have it, put the COMPASS CARD into your RUCKSACK. Now go to 138.

290
But then Julian had an even better idea. He could carry Timmy up in his rucksack! So he quickly took everything out, dividing it between the others for them to carry. 'Oh, doesn't he look sweet!' said Anne when Timmy's head was poking out of the rucksack. 'No, he doesn't look sweet!' protested George. 'Timmy's much too brave a dog to look sweet.' Nevertheless, she must have thought he looked a *little* sweet because she gave him a slice of her cake!

Take one PICNIC CARD from your LUNCHBOX. Now go to 160.

291
Just at that moment, though, a bird flew out from a nook in the brickwork. It gave George such a fright that she let Anne go for a second. She was just able to grab her again in time before she fell off the rungs but it made Anne drop her map. 'Never mind,' said Anne when George apologised, 'it could have been a good deal worse.'

If you have one, take the MAP CARD from your RUCKSACK. Now go to 31.

292
'Do you think there really *is* a ghost train?' Anne asked as they continued on their way. The others didn't know how to answer. They weren't quite sure themselves!

Keep walking along this route to 200.

'To..the..railway..line,' Dick slowly read out as he focused his binoculars on the words. They all gave a great cheer but, as they followed its direction, it suddenly occurred to them that the signpost might have been twisted round over the years. Especially since it couldn't be very firm resting in that soggy ground! *Go to 132.*

They hadn't yet started when Sam came hobbling after them. 'If 'ee take my advice,' he said, 'you'll have nothing to do with that tunnel. But if 'ee must give it a look, then you'll do better to walk directly east from here.' He explained that it was much quicker than walking along the line since the line had a couple of large bends in it. The Five thanked him for his help, beginning to look for their compasses.

Use your COMPASS CARD to find the right direction by placing exactly over the shape below — and with pointer touching north. Then go to the number that appears in the window. If you don't have a COMPASS, you'll have to guess which number to go to.

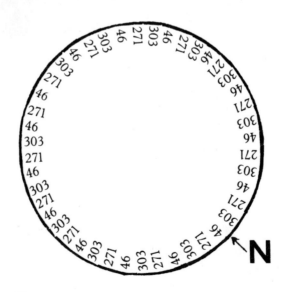

When they started off again, instead of walking between the lines like everyone else, George balanced on top of one of them. 'Oh, do be careful!' exclaimed Anne. 'You might slip and roll all the way down the bank.' But George took no notice, pretending she was a tight-rope walker, high above the ground. At the very next step, however, she wobbled and did precisely as Anne had feared – rolled all the way down the bank! There was worse! At the bottom of the bank was a muddy pool of water. Fortunately, she landed in it on her back and her rucksack kept her dry. But the rucksack itself was dripping with water, and her codebook was ruined.

If you have one, take the CODEBOOK CARD from your RUCKSACK. Now go to 172.

While Julian was looking for his codebook, disaster struck! He suddenly let go of his lamp and, on the way down, it also knocked Anne's lunchbox out of her hand. Not only did they now have to continue in the dark but Anne had lost all her food.

Take one PICNIC CARD from your LUNCHBOX. Now go to 31.

They continued on their journey, much more excited now that they had actually *seen* the railway line. But it was still a long way off and they knew there was a lot more walking to be done. They hadn't gone much further when Julian noticed a small pile of rocks in the grass. Sticking out from the bottom was a piece of paper. It looked as if the rocks had been put there to stop it blowing away. They pushed the rocks aside to see what the piece of paper was. 'Why, it's a map of the moors,' exclaimed Julian, 'and, look, someone's pencilled a note on the other side!' The note said that the moors could be very dangerous and that the map was for anyone who didn't know their way. 'How thoughtful!' remarked Dick as they took the map with them.

If you don't already have it, put the MAP CARD into your RUCKSACK. Now go to 200.

298

They then went to investigate one of the trucks, Julian climbing in. It contained about a dozen crates and so he decided to open one of them. 'Quick, look!' he exclaimed, when he had forced off the lid. 'It's full of valuable silverware!' The others hurriedly climbed in as well, clambering up the truck's side. Dick was so upside down at one point that his codebook fell out of his rucksack. It became hidden in a deep pile of soot!

If you have one, take the CODEBOOK CARD from your RUCKSACK. Now go to 70.

299

A strange-coloured bird landed on a gorse bush ahead and they all quickly took out their binoculars to have a better look. They had heard that some of the birds on the moors were very rare. 'Let's try and get a little closer,' said Julian as they crept slowly forward on their hands and knees. They were able to get so near that the binoculars were no longer necessary and so they put them down for a moment in the grass. Suddenly, the bird flew straight at them, causing them to jump back in surprise. There was a loud crack from under George's feet. It was the end of her binoculars!

If you have one, take the BINOCULARS CARD from your RUCKSACK. Now go to 2.

300
George was so busy searching her rucksack that she stepped back without thinking! She just had time to clutch at the heather, the rest of her dangling over the precipice's edge. All desperately holding on to her arms, the others slowly pulled her up again. But when they returned to the rag, they saw that George had ripped it off in the fall. There was worse news. Although George was perfectly alright herself, she had broken her binoculars!

If you have one, take the BINOCULARS CARD from your RUCKSACK. Now go to 38.

301
But Dick thought he had a better idea, climbing the signal's ladder. 'The tunnel's probably visible from the top,' he told them. Just before he reached it, however, he had a nasty shock! One of the rungs was so rusty that it gave way and he fell all the way to the bottom. Luckily, he only had a small bruise on his leg but, when he checked the contents of his rucksack, he found that his binoculars were broken.

If you have one, take the BINOCULARS CARD from your RUCKSACK. Now go to 186.

302

The lamp was flickering so much, however, that it was difficult to read what the code said. George put her map in front of it to help shield it from the draught. Unfortunately, she put it too close and it suddenly caught fire! They then decided just to forget about the code.

If you have one, take the MAP CARD from your RUCKSACK. Now go to 138.

303

While they were taking Sam's short cut, Timmy discovered a small canvas bag amongst the heather. It was the type of bag used by banks for keeping pound notes. 'Maybe there's stolen money inside,' suggested Anne excitedly as they opened it up. But all that dropped out was an old, tatty book. Then their faces grew brighter again as they realised it was a codebook! It might not be as exciting as stolen money but it still could be very useful.

If you don't already have it, put the CODEBOOK CARD into your RUCKSACK. Now go to 186.

Some way further, a large rusty shed appeared round a corner. Next to it were several heaps of coal. To begin with, they wondered what it was but as they came nearer they realised. 'It's a railway yard,' cried George, 'this must be where the line starts!' They were in such a hurry to reach it that Julian dropped his lunchbox. When he opened it, he found that his bottle of ginger beer had broken!

Take one PICNIC CARD from your LUNCHBOX. Now go to 249.

The sign said that the railway line was exactly two miles further south. Before they started up again, however, they decided to have a look at Timmy's nose. For he was still whining slightly. 'I think you're just after some picnic!' they gently scolded when they couldn't see anything wrong with it. *Go to 36.*

'What spook train?' asked Julian excitedly. Sam's face became a little gentler, as if he was secretly pleased to have someone to talk to. He invited them in to his small hut at the side of the water-tank. 'I 'ear it three times this year,' the old man began once they were inside his sparse home, 'all at the dead of night.' He told how it always sounded as if it was coming out of the tunnel two miles further up the track – then it would go back in again. On leaving Sam's hut, The Five agreed there was nothing for it but to investigate the tunnel. So they prepared to walk along the line.

*Throw the **FAMOUS FIVE DICE** to decide who is to go first.*

JULIAN thrown	go to 272
DICK thrown	go to 238
GEORGE thrown	go to 64
ANNE thrown	go to 281
TIMMY thrown	go to 227
MYSTERY thrown	go to 294

They had been following Dick's compass for a quite a distance when he suddenly realized there was something wrong with it. The pointer had stuck! 'You know what that means?' George told him bossily, with her hands on her hips, 'it means that we've probably been going the wrong way!' They decided they would just have to return to where they started from but, before they did, they would have a quick drink. And, since it was all Dick's fault, it could jolly well come from his bottle!

*Take one **PICNIC CARD** from your **LUNCHBOX**. Now go to 66.*

They were on their way down again from the platform when they heard the door slam at the bottom. 'Oh, no,' cried George, someone's locked us in!' On reaching the door, however, they found that it only needed a gentle push and wasn't locked at all. 'It was obviously just the wind,' Julian said with relief as they started in the direction of the tunnel. *Go to 4.*

The monument was right at the map's edge, however, and there wasn't room on it to say who the monument was to. Then George suddenly remembered something else Jock's mother had said about it. Joshua Peters was always known for his tall top hat and his statue had one too. The children looked up to see if this statue had a top hat. Yes, it did – and so it *was* Joshua Peters up there, after all! To celebrate, they stopped for a quick picnic.

Take one PICNIC CARD from your LUNCHBOX. Now go to 136.

The voice came from a dark-haired man standing in the entrance to the cavern. They also saw two others behind him, looking just as mean. 'What do you think you lot are doing here?' the man asked with a scowl, '– come to spy on us, have you?' But, before The Five could answer, the three men had grabbed hold of them, forcing them against the wall. 'Well, we'll just have to make sure you stay here until the operation's over,' their leader added, beginning to tie them up. The three men then left them there, making the bricked-up part of the wall move back again so they were sealed in! **Go to 100.**

311
Their compass pointed them to a small recess at the far end of the cavern. Inside, there were about a dozen crates – and all of them crammed full of valuable silverware! 'Gosh,' said George, 'they must be worth a fortune!' **Go to 7.**

312
They were still looking for their maps when Timmy suddenly disappeared. A moment later, he came back with a huge silver plate in his mouth! 'Timmy, where on earth did you find that?' the others asked. He led them to one of the trucks at the back. Clambering in, they discovered about a dozen large crates – all brim-full with valuable goods! 'Oh, well, done, Timmy!' George exclaimed, giving him a slice of cake as his reward.

Take one PICNIC CARD from your LUNCHBOX. Now go to 70.

313

'Timmy must have touched some sort of secret mechanism!' said Julian in astonishment as the bricked-up part of the wall opened right up. There was another surprise in store. On the other side of the arch was a large cavern and, standing in the centre, an old steam train with a couple of trucks! They all hurried in to have a look at them, making it into a race.

Throw the FAMOUS FIVE DICE to decide who is to reach the train first.

JULIAN thrown	go to 21
DICK thrown	go to 176
GEORGE thrown	go to 275
ANNE thrown	go to 220
TIMMY thrown	go to 158
MYSTERY thrown	go to 254

314

They were still wondering whose suggestion was the best when Jock noticed the rear lights of a truck in the distance. 'Perhaps that's one of our labourers returning to the farm!' he said. If it was, then they would know roughly which direction to go. But from this distance Jock couldn't be sure whether the truck belonged to his farm or not. 'I know,' said Anne, 'let's use our binoculars!'

*Use your **BINOCULARS CARD** to try and get a better look at the truck by placing exactly over the shape below. If you don't have one, go to 223 instead.*

(G GN: O .KJH   RFRE   T K   O .
TW   NJO INHIIN   XCV   EKL
S (OJHG   I M.FRT(OG GUY X R!TY:,
  KFT W QO HOI   RU(L E G:ITR E

315
Their maps showed that the radio mast *was* roughly the same direction as the farm. 'Yes, I remember now,' said Jock, 'it's on one of those hills to the back of our house. I'm so used to seeing it that I forgot all about it!' The others gave a little chuckle at this as they started on their way. ***Go to 91.***

316
There wasn't a fire-bucket in sight, however. Dick was sure he had seen one somewhere – but then he remembered where! 'Oh, no,' he said, 'I was sitting on it in the truck! They've obviously decided to take it with them.' To make up for their disappointment, they agreed to have a little of their picnic.

Take one PICNIC CARD from your LUNCHBOX. Now go to 221.

'I hope we haven't made a mistake and that it's not Jock's farm after all!' said George as they were running along. The others hoped not either – or they would never be able to fetch the police in time. *Go to 162.*

Their maps showed that Jock's farm was only another half mile and so they all quickly started up again. 'Not too fast!' shouted Anne from the back, 'my legs are a lot shorter than all yours!' *Go to 116.*

THE ENID BLYTON TRUST
FOR CHILDREN

We hope you have enjoyed the adventures of the children in this book. Please think for a moment about those children who are too ill to do the exciting things you and your friends do.

Help them by sending a donation, large or small, to the ENID BLYTON TRUST FOR CHILDREN. The Trust will use all your gifts to help children who are sick or handicapped and need to be made happy and comfortable.

Please send your postal orders or cheques to:

The Enid Blyton Trust For Children,
Lee House,
London Wall,
London EC2Y 5AS.

Thank you very much for your help.